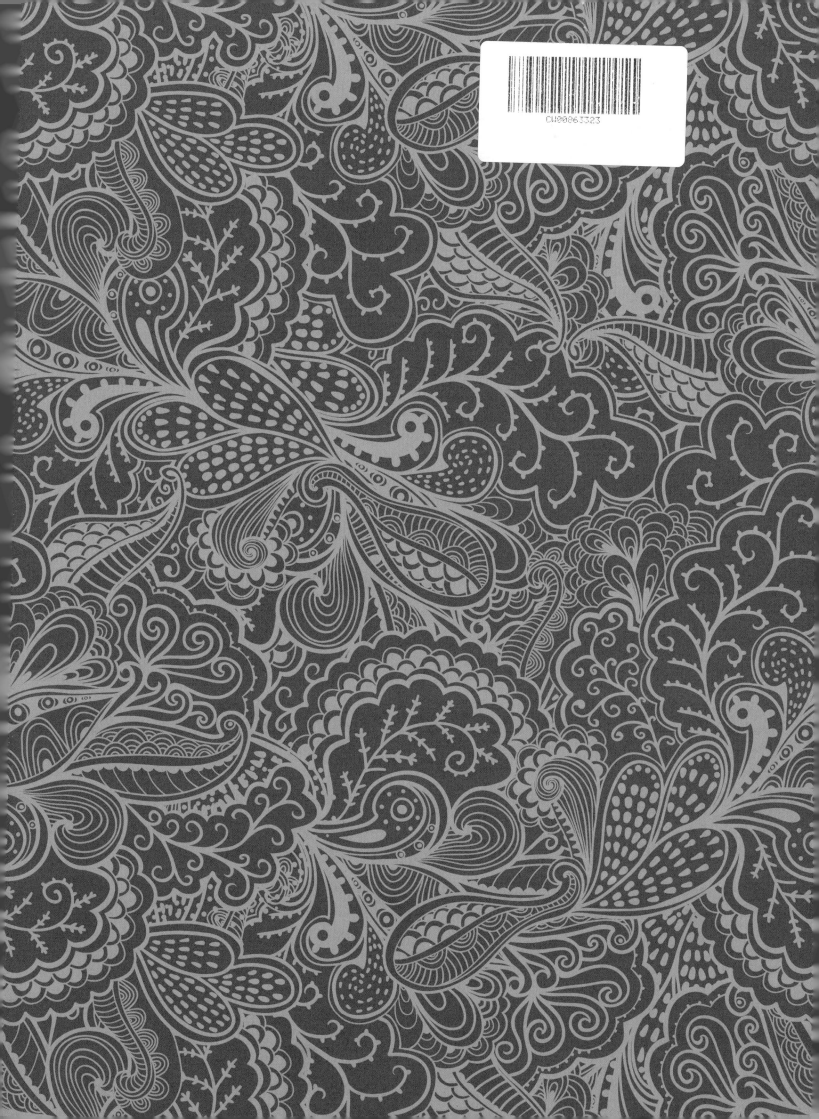

This book belongs to

Ruby and Abbie

Love from Auntie George and Uncle Mark.
Happy Christmas! xxx

Illustrated Treasury of
Princess Stories

Compiled by Vic Parker

Miles
Kelly

First published in 2015 by Miles Kelly Publishing Ltd
Harding's Barn, Bardfield End Green, Thaxted, Essex, CM6 3PX, UK

Copyright © Miles Kelly Publishing Ltd 2015

This edition published 2016

2 4 6 8 10 9 7 5 3 1

Publishing Director Belinda Gallagher
Creative Director Jo Cowan
Editorial Director Rosie Neave
Editor Amy Johnson
Designers Jo Cowan, Joe Jones
Cover Designer Jo Cowan
Production Elizabeth Collins, Caroline Kelly
Reprographics Stephan Davis, Jennifer Cozens, Thom Allaway

ISBN 978-1-78209-986-4

Printed in China

British Library Cataloguing-in-Publication Data
A catalogue record for this book is available from the British Library

ACKNOWLEDGEMENTS

The publishers would like to thank the following artists
who have contributed to this book:
Cover: Sylvia Vivanco (Astound)
Inside pages: Ellie Jenkins, Natalia Moore (Advocate Art);
Rosie Butcher, Louise Ellis (The Bright Agency);
Giada Negri, Natascia Ugliano (Milan Illustrations Agency);
Mónica Carretero (Plum Pudding Illustration Agency)

Made with paper from a sustainable forest

www.mileskelly.net

CONTENTS

- -

SEALED WITH A KISS

DAMSELS IN DISTRESS

BRAVE, WISE AND TRUE

MAGICAL MAIDENS

ABOUT THE AUTHORS

Learn more about some of the famous authors behind these much-loved stories.

Jacob and Wilhelm Grimm
1785–1863 and 1786–1859

The Grimm brothers were born near Frankfurt, Germany. While at university, they developed an interest in traditional tales, which became a lifelong passion. While working as librarians and university researchers, they collected and published over 200 folk and fairytales. Over the years, the stories have been rewritten and adapted countless times.

Snow White • Sleeping Beauty • The Princess and the Frog • The Goose-girl
The Twelve Dancing Princesses

Hans Christian Andersen
1805–1875

Born into a poor family in Denmark, Andersen was apprenticed to a weaver and a tailor. He then worked as an actor before turning to writing. Andersen became famous for his fairytales, which are still much loved today. They have inspired many works including songs and films.

The Princess and the Swineherd • The Princess and the Pea
The Wild Swans • The Little Mermaid

Alexander Afanasev
1826–1871

Afanasev was a Russian librarian who was inspired by the Brothers Grimm. He studied law at Moscow University and later dedicated himself to collecting nearly 600 Russian folk tales and fairytales, which were compiled between 1855 and 1864. These were published in eight instalments, which together comprised one of the largest collections of traditional tales in the world.

The Princess who Would Not Smile

Andrew Lang
1844–1912

Born in Selkirk, Scotland, Lang studied Classics (ancient Greek and Latin literature) and then became a journalist, poet, novelist and critic. He had a lifelong love of folklore, magic and myth. Lang is best-known today for collecting and adapting hundreds of folk tales and fairytales from all over the world in a 'Fairy Book' series for children.

The Princess on the Glass Mountain • The Princess who was Hidden Underground • The White Wolf • The Dirty Shepherdess • The Princess Bear

About the Authors

Yei Theodora Ozaki
1871–1932

Yei Theodora Ozaki was the daughter of a Japanese father and a British mother. Her father was a baron, and one of the first Japanese men to study in the West. Ozaki worked as a teacher and secretary and spent years travelling between Europe and Japan, before marrying a Japanese politician. She translated many Japanese short stories and fairytales into English.

The Bamboo-cutter and the Moonchild

Flora Annie Steel
1847–1929

Born Flora Annie Webster in Middlesex, England, at age 20 she married Henry William Steel, a member of the Indian civil service. For the next 22 years she lived in India, where she became a school inspector. The birth of her daughter gave her a chance to become involved with local women and learn their language. She gathered their folk tales, a collection of which was published in 1894.

Princess Pepperina

E Nesbit
1858–1924

Nesbit was born in London, England. She had five children, and wrote poems, articles and children's stories to earn money. However, she used the initial 'E' rather than her full name, 'Edith', to disguise the fact that she was a woman. She wrote more than forty books for children, and created the idea of mixing real-life characters and settings with magical elements.

Melisande

Katharine Pyle
1863–1938

Pyle lived in Wilmington, Delaware, USA. She studied art and worked as an illustrator before becoming well-known as a writer of short stories, poems and plays for children. She also compiled and retold several volumes of fairytales and myths. Pyle continued to illustrate the work of others (including her brother, Howard), as well as painting portraits.

The Princess and the Demon

ABOUT THE ARTISTS

Rosie Butcher dreamed of drawing the pictures in children's books since she was very young. She is extremely dedicated to illustration and spends her time exploring and developing her skills. She works in a number of mediums, both traditional and digital.

The Fair One with Locks of Gold • Sleeping Beauty • The Princess and the Pea • The Princess who was Hidden Underground • The White Wolf The Princess Bear

Mónica Carretero was born in Madrid and now lives in the beautiful city of Segovia in Spain. She describes her head as a cabin crowded with characters all wanting to know when she is going to tell their stories and draw them. Mónica loves her job, and also enjoys running and cooking.

The Princess on the Glass Mountain • Melisande • The Wild Swans The Twelve Dancing Princesses

Louise Ellis is passionate about children's books, and has been creating art from a very young age. She works traditionally, using acrylics, watercolours, pencils, texture paste and collage to create her detailed, imaginative and playful illustrations.

Page decoration • The Princess and the Frog

About the Artists

Ellie Jenkins lives and works in her home city of Bristol. She has illustrated picture books, poetry, greetings cards and packaging. Ellie takes inspiration from her environment, in particular trees, animals and buildings.

Princess Chatterbox • The Fair Fiorita • The Goose-girl • The Princess and the Hero • Princess Pepperina

Natalia Moore is a qualified art teacher and freelance illustrator. She works with mixed media and adds the finishing touches digitally. Natalia likes to draw from real-life and is never without her sketchbook.

The Bamboo-cutter and the Moonchild • The Princess and the Swineherd • The Princess who Would Not Smile • The Little Red Princess of the Forest • The Three Daughters of King O'Hara

Giada Negri was born by Lake Como in Italy, where she now works and lives with her husband and little boy. She has never stopped drawing and designing since she was a child. Her work has been published by renowned Italian publishers, and she has also taken part in several art exhibitions.

How the Princess was Beaten in a Race • Little Daylight • The Princess who was Stolen • The Little Mermaid • The Princess and the Demon

Natascia Ugliano is a graduate of the Academy of Fine Arts of Brera in Milan, Italy. She has worked as a set designer and costume design assistant for both theatre and cinema. Since 2005, she has been a freelance illustrator for several publishers, both in Italy and abroad.

Snow White • Andromeda and the Sea Monster • The Dirty Shepherdess • The Tsarevna Frog

THE FAIREST OF THEM ALL

Snow White

Retold from the Grimm brothers'
version of a German fairytale

In the middle of winter, when broad flakes of snow were falling, a queen sat sewing at her window. As she sewed, she accidentally pricked her finger and three drops of blood fell out of the window and onto the snow on the windowsill. She gazed upon it thoughtfully and said, "I wish for a daughter as white as snow, as red as blood, and as black as ebony!" Soon after she had a little girl who really did

Snow White

grow up like this. Her skin was as white as snow, her lips as red as blood, and her hair as black as ebony. Her name was Snow White.

Sadly, the queen died when the princess was young, and the king soon married again. His new wife was very beautiful, but so vain that she could not bear to think that anyone was handsomer than her. She had a magic looking-glass, to which she would go and say:

"Tell me, glass, tell me true!
Of all the ladies in the land,
Who is fairest, tell me, who?"

And the glass had always answered:

"Thou, queen, art the fairest in all the land."

Upon hearing this, the queen was satisfied.

Meanwhile, Snow White grew more and more beautiful. By the time she turned seventeen, she was as bright as the day.

Snow White

One day, the glass answered the queen:

"Thou, queen, art fair, and beauteous to see,
But Snow White is lovelier far than thee!"

When the queen heard this, she turned pale with rage and envy. She called for one of her servants at once. "Take Snow White out into the wild woods and kill her!" she ordered.

The servant did as he was told and took Snow White deep into the wild woods. But he could not bear to hurt her. Instead, he left her there, hoping that someone would find her – before the wild beasts tore her to pieces.

Poor Snow White wandered alone through the woods and deep into the mountains, full of fear. The wild beasts roared about her, but not one did her any harm. In the evening she came to a cottage. There was no one at home but the door was unlocked, and so she went in to rest, for her feet would carry her no further.

Everything was clean and neat inside the cottage. On the table was a white cloth, and laid out on it were seven little plates, seven little loaves, seven little glasses with wine in them, and seven knives and forks. By the wall stood seven little beds.

As Snow White was very hungry, she took a little piece of one of the loaves and drank a little wine from one of the glasses. After that she decided to lie down and rest. So she picked one of the little beds and exhausted, fell straight to sleep.

By and by, in came the owners of the cottage. They were seven dwarfs, who lived by mining in the mountains for gold. They lit the lamps, and cried out with wonder and astonishment as the light fell across the

sleeping Snow White.

"Good heavens!" one gasped.

"How beautiful she is!" breathed another.

They were all very glad to see her, and took care not to wake her. The seventh dwarf, whose bed Snow White was sleeping in, spent all night on the floor by her bedside.

In the morning, when Snow White woke up, she told the dwarfs her story. Their hearts were filled with pity, and they insisted that the young princess stay in the cottage with them, promising to look after her. Then they went out to do their day's work, seeking out gold in the mountains. But before they left, they warned Snow White: "The queen may find out where you are, so take care and let no one in."

Back at the castle, the queen gleefully thought that Snow White was dead. Believing herself to be the most beautiful in the land once more, she went to her looking-glass and asked it eagerly:

"Tell me, glass, tell me true!
Of all the ladies in the land,
Who is fairest, tell me, who?"

And the glass answered:

"Thou, queen, art the fairest in all this land:
But over the hills, in the greenwood shade,
Where seven dwarfs their dwelling have made,
There Snow White is hiding her head, and she
Is lovelier far, O queen, than thee."

The wicked queen was furious, for she knew that the servant had betrayed her. She shook with rage and hissed, "Snow White shall die!" She went at once into her chamber and, using an evil spell, prepared an apple which was poisonous on one side. The fruit looked rosy and tempting, but whoever tasted the poisonous half was sure to die.

She then disguised herself as an old pedlar woman and travelled into the mountains to the dwarfs' cottage. She knocked at the door, but Snow White put her head out of the window and said, "I dare not let anyone in, for the dwarfs have told me not to."

"Do as you please," said the old woman, "but at any rate take this pretty apple."

"No," said Snow White, "I dare not take it."

"You silly girl!" answered the old woman. "What are you afraid of? Do you think it is poisoned? Come! You eat one half and I will eat the other." The old woman took a big bite from one side of the apple and then offered it to Snow White. The apple looked so rosy and juicy that Snow White was very tempted, and when she saw the old woman eat, she took it eagerly. But she had scarcely bitten into the apple when she fell down dead! The queen hurried back to the castle, her wicked heart filled with joy.

When evening came and the dwarfs arrived home, they were horrified to find Snow White dead upon the ground. They laid

her upon a bier and wept and wailed for three whole days. Yet her cheeks stayed rosy and her face looked just as it did while she was alive.

"We will never bury her in the cold ground," the dwarfs decided. They made a coffin of glass, so that they might still look at her, and wrote upon it in gold letters what her name was, and that she was a king's daughter. They set the coffin in a little clearing among the trees, and one of the dwarfs always sat nearby to watch over it.

There Snow White lay for a long, long time – still only looking as though she was asleep... At last, one morning a prince came riding through the forest and saw the beautiful princess lying in the glass coffin. She was so enchanting, he could not resist stooping to give her a kiss. But as the prince lifted the lid of the coffin and gently raised her head, the piece of apple fell from between her lips. Snow White suddenly woke. "Where am I?" she said.

"You are quite safe with me," the prince replied. He was overjoyed, as were the dwarfs when they saw Snow White alive again.

The prince took Snow White back to his palace, where they were married amid joyous celebrations. As for the wicked queen, when her magic looking-glass told her that Snow White was alive once more and the fairest of them all, she choked with rage and fell down dead. So Snow White and her prince lived and reigned happily for many, many years, often travelling up into the mountains to visit their best friends, the dwarfs.

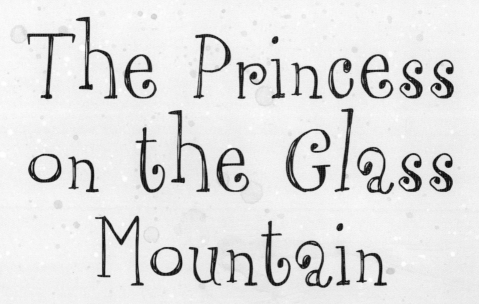

The Princess on the Glass Mountain

Retold from Andrew Lang's version of a Polish fairytale

Once upon a time there was a glass mountain. At the top stood a castle made of pure gold, and in front of the castle there was a tree on which grew golden apples.

It was said that anyone who could pick a golden apple could enter the castle. Inside it, in a silver room, sat an enchanted princess. She was dazzlingly beautiful, and also wondrously rich, for the castle cellars were piled high with great chests full of gold and precious jewels.

Many knights had come to try their luck, but not one had managed to reach the tree of golden apples. The knights were brave and determined, and all had bold, strong horses with spiked horseshoes. But no one was able to get more than halfway up the steep glass mountain before sliding back down and crashing to the bottom. Sometimes the young men broke an arm, sometimes a leg, and sometimes even their neck. Often their horses were horribly injured. The worst-hurt riders and their steeds ended up groaning and dying around the foot of the treacherous mountain, and there their bodies lay.

With great sadness, the princess sat at her window and watched the daring knights trying to reach her on their splendid horses.

Talk of her beauty spread far and wide, sparking courage in scores of young men in distant countries. They flocked from the four corners of the earth to try to reach the princess and break the enchantment that kept her prisoner in the castle. But they all failed.

The closest attempt came one day when a knight in golden armour galloped on a mighty stallion towards the mountain. He spurred on his horse and made a rush at the gleaming glass. Sparks of fire flew from the horse's hooves, and it trod on the glass as if it had been level earth! Many other knights were watching and they gazed in astonishment, for the golden knight very nearly reached the top… But suddenly, a huge eagle rose up with its mighty wings spread, hitting the knight's horse in the eye. The beast shied and reared up high in the air. Its hind hooves slipped and it tumbled with its rider down the steep mountainside, joining the many battered and lifeless bodies littering the mud at the bottom.

After seven long years, a farmer's son arrived one day at the foot of the glass mountain. He had no armour and no horse. However, he was fit and strong, and had a good, brave heart. He had listened to his parents speak of the beautiful princess for a long time, and had finally decided to try his own luck. He had gone into the forest and trapped and killed a ferocious wild cat. Then he had cut off the creature's sharp claws and carried them with him to the glass mountain.

Now he sat and bound them fast to his own arms and feet.

Looking about, he could clearly see how many knights had died in attempting this feat, but he did not feel afraid. When he was ready, he strode boldly up to the steep mountain on foot and began to climb…

By the time the sun began to set, the youth had not got more than halfway up. He was so exhausted he could hardly breathe and his mouth was parched with thirst. A huge black cloud passed over his head and he begged it to let a drop of water fall on him, but it just sailed past.

The young man's feet were torn and bleeding, and he could now only hold on with his hands. Dusk was gathering – he peered upwards through the gloom but he could not glimpse the top of the mountain. Yet when he looked down, he could still make out the twisted bodies sprawled below.

It was soon pitch dark and only the stars lit up the glass mountain. The poor boy could no longer struggle to get higher, for all his strength had left him. He just clung on to the glassy slope as if he had glue on his bloodstained hands.

Now, the golden apple tree was guarded by the eagle which had overthrown the golden knight and his horse. Every night it flew around the glass mountain, keeping a careful look-out. No sooner had the moon emerged from the clouds than the great bird rose up into the air and circled round, quickly catching sight of the farmer's son.

The eagle was hungry and could see that the lad was weak and helpless. It swooped down upon the boy and dug its sharp claws

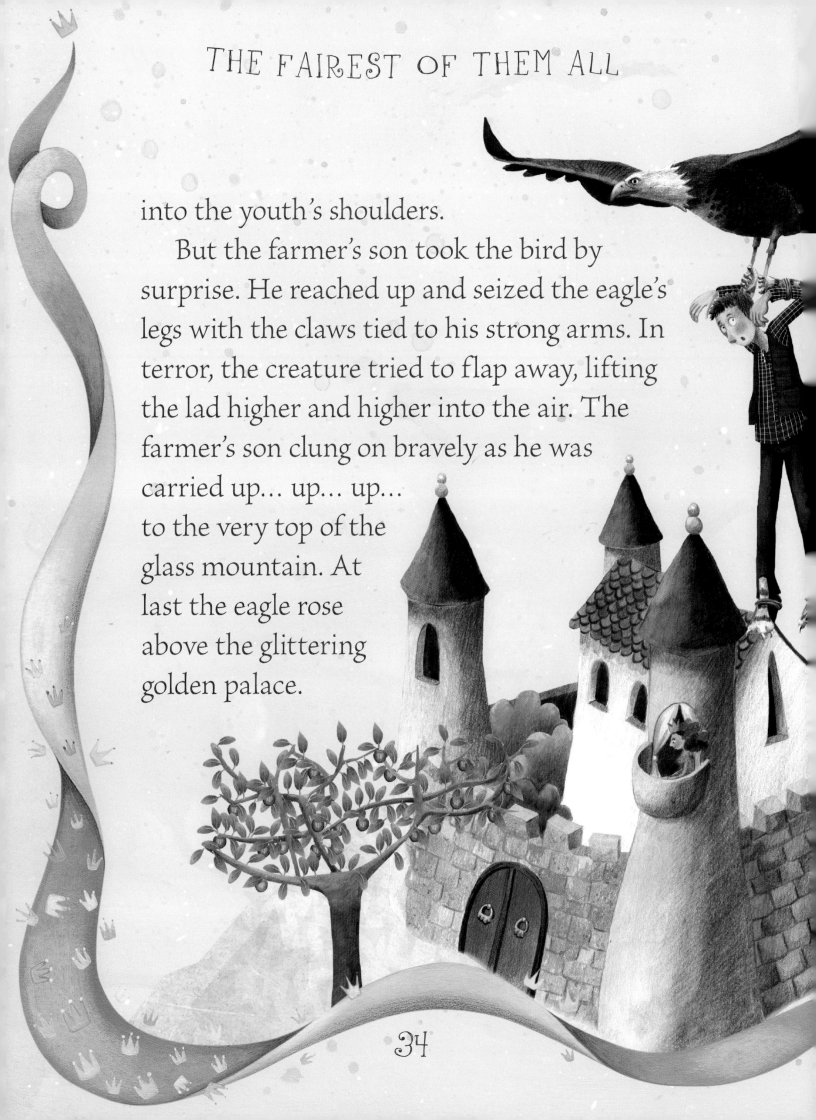

into the youth's shoulders.

But the farmer's son took the bird by surprise. He reached up and seized the eagle's legs with the claws tied to his strong arms. In terror, the creature tried to flap away, lifting the lad higher and higher into the air. The farmer's son clung on bravely as he was carried up… up… up… to the very top of the glass mountain. At last the eagle rose above the glittering golden palace.

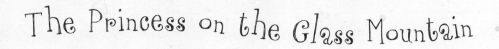

Round one of its high windows was a balcony in which the princess sat, lost in thought. How beautiful she looked – but how sad!

The young man realized he was being carried near to the apple tree. He released his grip on the eagle's legs and the relieved bird soared away, vanishing into the clouds. Meanwhile, the youth tumbled into the broad branches. Trembling with excitement, he untied the claws from his arms and feet. Then he picked several of the stunning golden apples and put them in his pocket. He climbed down from the tree, drew a deep breath, and approached the castle.

To his dismay, in front of the doors there suddenly appeared a huge, snarling dragon. He hastily threw a golden apple at it – and the beast vanished! At the same moment, the castle doors swung

open. Beyond, the farmer's son could see a courtyard full of beautiful flowers and trees. And out came the princess, running towards him. She wept with happiness and gratitude as she thanked him for breaking the spell that had kept her prisoner.

"Look!" she exclaimed, and she took his hand and led him to the edge of the glass mountain. The farmer's son peered down and could just make out, to his great astonishment, a mass of horses and men all milling around at its foot. "All the knights and horses who were injured or who died trying to rescue me have been healed, and have come back to life!" the princess cried joyfully.

So the people of many kingdoms celebrated when the princess and the farmer's son were married. And the youth became a good and fair ruler alongside his very beautiful queen.

The Fair One with Locks of Gold

Retold from Hamilton, Wright and Mabie's version
of a French fairytale by Madame d'Aulnoy

There was once a most beautiful princess, who was known as the Fair One with Locks of Gold. Her hair shone like the sun and flowed all the way down to her feet, and she always wore a coronet of beautiful flowers and pearls and diamonds.

A rich young king from a neighbouring land had sent an ambassador to ask for her hand in marriage. The ambassador was dressed in the finest clothes, and surrounded by servants on beautiful horses laiden down with gifts. However, the princess was not impressed, and the ambassador returned to the king with a message from her saying, "No thank you".

All the people in the kingdom were most disappointed. The king was downcast – and annoyed too! When his courtiers saw how upset he was, one of them spoke up. "Your Majesty, I believe if you sent me to the Fair One with Locks of Gold, I could bring her back for you." It was a young man called Avenant, who was so handsome and charming that everybody loved him.

"Would you really try?" asked the king, brightening.

"Of course," smiled Avenant. "All I need is a good horse and a letter with your seal upon it, so the princess knows you have sent me."

The king was delighted. So at dawn, Avenant left the palace with his faithful talking dog, Cabriole, trotting by his side.

The pair travelled until they came to a meadow, where they sat down by a stream for a few moments' rest. Suddenly Avenant noticed a large golden carp wriggling around on the bank, gasping for air. He realized that the fish must have leapt out of the water by mistake, and hurried to throw it back in.

To Avenant's huge surprise, the relieved creature spoke to him. "Thank you for your kindness," it said. "One day I will reward you." Then the carp dived down and was gone.

Avenant and Cabriole continued on their journey. After a few hours, Avenant saw up in the sky a huge eagle hunting a terrified crow. Quickly the courtier took his bow and shot an arrow through the eagle so it fell to the ground, dead. "You have saved my life," panted the crow, alighting on a tree, "and one day I will do you a good turn likewise."

Again, Avenant and Cabriole went on their way. By the time night fell, they found themselves in a wood, where they heard an owl crying out despairingly. They searched about and came upon the little owl trapped in a bird-catcher's net. Avenant drew his knife and cut the threads at once. "Thank you for setting me free," sighed the owl, "I will always remember your kindness."

Finally, Avenant and Cabriole arrived at the castle that was home to the Fair One with Locks of Gold. When they were shown in to see the princess, Avenant was struck still by her beauty, scarcely able to speak. But then he recovered himself and began to sing the king's praises. He did it so winningly that all the ladies-in-waiting fell in love – though not with the king, with Avenant himself!

His words even softened the princess's heart. For when he begged her to return with him, she said, "Gentle Avenant, I assure you, I would rather say 'yes' to you than to any other. But alas, about a month ago I accidentally dropped my ring into the river. I vowed not to marry anyone unless it is found."

Avenant went away most dejected, for he was sure that the princess had given him an impossible task. He tossed and turned all night, worrying. But when day came, Cabriole told him, "My dear master, do not despair. Let us go to the riverside."

Avenant smiled at his faithful companion and took the little dog's advice. No sooner had they reached the river when they heard a voice

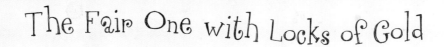

calling, "Avenant! Avenant!"

Cabriole peered into the water and cried in amazement, "You won't believe this – it's the golden carp!"

"Here is the ring belonging to the Fair One with Locks of Gold," the fish announced, dropping it into Avenant's hand. Avenant gave the fish a thousand thanks and hurried back to the castle.

When the princess saw her ring, she was overjoyed.

"Oh thank you, Avenant, that's wonderful!" she cried. "But alas, I live under another vow. A terrible giant is terrorizing my country and I will not marry until he is dead." The princess was extremely impressed when Avenant set out to kill the giant at once.

On nearing the giant's castle, Avenant was horrified to see that the road was strewn with the bones of men he had devoured. When the giant saw the bold young man coming, he strode out to meet him, swinging his mighty spiked mace. He would surely have mashed Avenant to pieces if a crow hadn't suddenly flown at the giant and pecked at his eyes. While the giant was busy trying to beat away the bird, Avenant attacked with his sword and hacked off the giant's head.

"Now I have repaid your kindness," squawked the crow, for it was the bird

Avenant had saved from the eagle. Avenant gave him a thousand thanks and rode away.

"Behold, your enemy is dead," Avenant told the princess, showing her the giant's ugly head. "And now, I hope, you will no longer refuse my master the king."

The princess thought that Avenant was the bravest young man she had ever met. "Alas!" she sighed, "I must still refuse – unless you can enter the Cave of Doom and bring me the magical Water of Beauty!"

"Madam," said Avenant, "you are so beautiful that you do not need this water. However, I will go in search of it for you." And he set off once more.

Avenant travelled a long way to the top of the mountain where the Cave of Doom lay. The cave was guarded by a monstrous dragon, which came lumbering out when Avenant

approached, spewing fire and flexing his
razor-sharp claws.

"Avenant! Avenant!" came an urgent
whisper. The courtier looked around and saw
a little owl sitting on a branch. "You once
rescued me," the bird said, "now give me your

flask and let me go and fetch the Water of Beauty for you."

Gladly, Avenant gave the owl his flask. The little bird flew straight over the mighty dragon, quite unnoticed, into the cave. In a matter of minutes, the owl was back with the flask filled quite to the brim. Avenant was overjoyed at his good fortune. He gave the owl a thousand thanks, and returned with a merry heart to the city.

By this time, the Fair One with Locks of Gold had fallen quite in love with the gallant Avenant, and had nothing further to say. She commanded that all her belongings were to be packed, and in due course she set out with the courtier and his little dog back to their kingdom. 'Oh, if only I could marry you, Avenant,' the princess often thought to herself on the journey.

At length they arrived at the king's castle, and he came out to meet the Fair One with Locks of Gold with the richest presents in the world. The couple were soon married, but the princess was not happy. In fact, she was very miserable – unless she was in the company of Avenant, when she seemed bright and joyful.

Everyone, including the king, soon realized that the princess was in love with Avenant, not him. The king became so jealous that his heart was filled with hatred. He had Avenant thrown into the great tower, never to be released. When the princess sobbed and wrung her hands and begged the king to show mercy, his heart just hardened still further.

The king decided that if he were more handsome, the princess might love him after all. So he made up his mind to wash his face with the Water of Beauty. However, the king had no idea that one of the queen's maids had dropped the flask and spilt all of the water. The maid had replaced it with a liquid that looked just like the Water of Beauty – but which was actually a strong sleeping potion.

So the king washed his face with the liquid… and again… and again. He rubbed so much of the potion into his skin that he fell into a deep slumber – so deep that he stopped breathing and died.

Then Cabriole hurried straight to fetch the queen, who in turn dashed to the great tower and released Avenant. She put the king's crown upon his head and the royal cloak around his shoulders. "Now, at last, you will be my king," she announced.

Their wedding was the most splendid ever seen. Everyone in the kingdom was overjoyed to have the brave, handsome Avenant for their ruler. And the Fair One with Locks of Gold lived a very long time with her beloved Avenant and their faithful little dog Cabriole, happy and content.

How the Princess was Beaten in a Race

By Horace E Scudder

There was once a king who had an enchantingly beautiful daughter – so beautiful that every prince in all the countries around wished to marry her. The princess was also a very swift runner. She ran so fast that no one could overtake her.

The king was very proud of his beautiful, talented daughter and he loved her very much – he was in no hurry for her to get married and leave him. So he made an announcement that she would only marry a man who could beat her in a race. The first man to do so would have her for a wife. But whoever raced with her and did not beat her must have his head cut off.

At first there were many men who came to the palace to try their luck. After all, there were a great many princes who wanted to marry the beautiful princess. There was also a huge number of men who were not princes, but who also wanted to win the princess's hand in marriage.

The contest was fine fun for the girl. She raced with each and every man in turn, and she always won. Unfortunately, a great many heads were cut off as a result. So there came a time when it was hard to find anyone who dared to race with her.

Now, far off in the countryside there lived a very poor young man who thought to himself: 'I do not own anything, so I have only my head to lose if I do not win the race. However, if I should win I would become noble, and all my family would be noble too. We would never have to worry about money again. I think I will try.'

This young man was a very good runner and he was also extremely clever. He had heard that the princess was very fond of roses, so he gathered a fine posy. Next, he borrowed money from his friends. He had a gorgeous silken belt made, embroidered in shimmering threads. Then he bought a silken bag and placed in it a golden ball with some words painted on it in silver.

The young man tucked the posy, the belt and the ball in the bag into his pockets, and

THE FAIREST OF THEM ALL

went and knocked at the palace gate. When the porter answered, he told him he wished to race with the princess.

The princess herself was looking out of the window and heard what was said. She saw that the young man was poor and shabbily dressed, and she looked on him with scorn. But the king's law made no distinction between rich and poor, prince and peasant, so the princess made ready to run. The king and all the court gathered to see the race, and the executioner went off to sharpen his axe.

So the race began... The two had not run far, and the princess was easily outrunning the young man, when he drew out his bunch of roses and threw it at the feet of the princess. She stopped to pick it up, and was greatly pleased with the flowers. She looked at them, touched their velvety petals, smelt them, and began to tuck them into her hair. She had quite forgotten about the race when suddenly she noticed the young man far ahead of her.

At once she threw the flowers away, and ran like the wind to catch him up.

Before long, the swift princess overtook the young man. She tapped him lightly on the shoulder and said: "Stop, foolish boy! Do you hope to marry a princess?"

But as she sped past him, he threw before her the silken belt. Again she stopped, and stooped to look at it. It was a beautiful belt and she admired it greatly, clasping it about her waist. As she was buckling it, she suddenly caught sight of the young man well on towards the finish line. "Wretch!" she cried, and burst into angry tears. She flung the belt away and bounded forward, her legs soon covering the ground between them.

Once more, the princess caught up with the young man. She seized him by the arm. "You shall not marry me!" she exclaimed angrily, and sprang past him. She was nearing the finish line, but the young man now let fall at her feet the silken bag. The golden ball glittered inside it and the princess was curious to see what it was. She paused for just a moment, raised the bag from the ground and took out the ball. She saw it had letters on it and she stood still to read them:

WHO PLAYS WITH ME
SHALL NEVER TIRE OF PLAY.

"I should like to see if that is true," said the princess thoughtfully, and she began to play with the ball. She threw it again and again, laughing as it glinted in the sun. No one can say if she would have eventually grown tired of it, for suddenly she heard a great shout. The young man had reached the finish line!

His head was safe. He and his family were made noble, he married the princess, and in time they had children who were the fastest runners in seventy-seven kingdoms.

The Bamboo-cutter and the Moonchild

Retold from Yei Theodora Ozaki's
version of a Polish fairytale

Long ago, there was an old man who made a living by cutting bamboo, which his wife wove into useful items like baskets to sell. The couple were very poor – and sad also, for Heaven had never sent them a child.

One morning, the old man was out in the bamboo forest as usual when suddenly the grove was flooded with a strange green light. Looking round in astonishment, he saw that

the brilliance was streaming from one
bamboo in particular. The old man dropped
his axe and went to take a closer look. He saw
that the light came from a hollow in the
green stem in which stood
a tiny girl, exquisitely
beautiful.

"You must have been sent to be my child," said the old man, quite delighted. And he took the girl home to his wife. Now at last the old couple were happy – and they showered their beautiful, mysterious child with love.

Over the days that followed, when the old man was cutting the bamboo, he often found gold in the notches of the stems – and precious stones also. The couple were suddenly rich! The old man built them a fine house and was no longer known as the poor bamboo-cutter, but as a wealthy man.

Three months passed, and in that time the bamboo child miraculously became a full-grown girl. She seemed to be magic – anyone who felt troubled discovered that their worries vanished and they became happy once they had seen her. The family's house was always filled with a soft glow, so that even in the dark of night it was as light as day. The old couple called in a famous name-giver and he gave her the name of Princess Moonlight, for he said that she must have been a daughter of the Moon God himself.

Princess Moonlight was of such wondrous beauty that everyone declared there had never been anyone so lovely. The princess's fame spread far and wide, and many young men journeyed to win her hand. A crowd of suitors gathered eagerly outside the house. They waited for days… and weeks… and months… but the old couple did not let any of them see Princess Moonlight.

Gradually, the young men gave up and went home – all except five knights who stood outside the house, come rain or shine, vowing never to leave until they had seen the princess. The bamboo-cutter was impressed by their determination and took pity on them. After all, he was anxious to see his daughter happily married before he died. He advised his daughter that she should choose one of these five worthy young men to be her husband.

Princess Moonlight had no wish to be married. Yet she did not want to displease her father either. She said that she would meet the five young men – if each could bring her something she desired from a distant country. The first knight was to fetch the stone bowl that had belonged to Buddha in India. The second knight was to go to the Mountain of Horai, near the Eastern Sea, and bring her a branch from the wonderful gold and silver tree that grew on its summit. The third knight was told to go to China and search for the fire-rat and to bring her its skin. The fourth knight was told to search for the dragon that carried on its head the stone that shone with five colours, and to bring that very stone to her. The fifth knight was to find the swallow that carried a shell in its stomach and to bring the shell to her.

The old man thought that these were impossible tasks. But the five knights all bravely resolved to try and get what she desired of them.

The first knight sent word to the princess that he was starting out that very day. However, he had not the courage to go all the way to India, for in those days travelling was very difficult and full of danger. So he went to a temple in Kyoto and paid a priest a large sum of money for a stone bowl from the altar there. He then wrapped it carefully in a cloth of gold and, after waiting for three years, returned and gave it to the old man.

Princess Moonlight took the bowl from its gold wrapping, expecting it to fill the room with light. But it did not shine at all, so she knew that it was not the true bowl of Buddha. She returned it and refused to see him, and the knight went back to his home in despair.

The second knight got halfway to the Eastern Sea, then decided he'd had enough. He sent his servants home and instead paid skilful jewellers to make him a gold and silver branch. Then he journeyed to the bamboo-cutter and tried to make himself look worn out with travel.

Princess Moonlight took the branch in her hand and looked at it carefully. She knew it was impossible for the knight to have obtained a branch from the gold and silver tree growing on Mount Horai so quickly, and she sent him home in disgrace.

The third knight had a friend in China, so he wrote to him and promised him a fortune in gold if he could send him the skin of the fire-rat. When it arrived, he put it carefully in a box and hurried to the bamboo-cutter.

Princess Moonlight put the skin to the test. She knew that if it were the real thing it would not burn. So she threw the skin into the fire – it crackled and burnt up at once! The princess knew that this man had not fulfilled his quest either.

The fourth knight called all his servants together and gave them the order to seek the dragon and its jewel far and wide. He strictly forbade any of them to return till they had found it. However, his servants simply took a holiday. They went to all sorts of pleasant places together, laughing about their master's impossible command.

As for the fifth knight – he travelled to the ends of the earth in his quest. But try as he might, he could not find the swallow's shell. In fact, as far as I know, he is still looking...

Meanwhile, news of Princess Moonlight's beauty had reached the ears of the mighty Emperor of Japan. While on a hunting trip in the area of the bamboo-cutter's house, he went to see the princess for himself.

Never had the emperor seen anyone so wonderfully beautiful. He could hardly look upon Princess Moonlight, for she shone with beauty! The emperor fell deeply in love with her and begged her to come to his court, where he would give her everything she could wish for.

But the princess stopped him. She said if she were forced to go to the palace she would turn at once into a shadow – and even as she spoke, her figure began to fade. Quickly, the emperor promised to leave her there if only she would come back, which she did.

So the emperor left the house with a heavy heart. Princess Moonlight was for him the most enchanting woman in the world. He thought of her night and day and wrote her many letters, to which Princess Moonlight wrote sweet replies.

But then one night Princess Moonlight and her parents were sitting on their balcony, when a strange cloud formed around the moon. It rolled slowly earthwards, nearer and nearer, until it hovered in front of the house, close to the ground. In the midst of the cloud there stood a chariot filled with bright spirits. One, who was clearly the king, announced, "The time has come for Princess Moonlight to return to the moon – from where she indeed came. We know what good care you have taken of her – we rewarded you by putting the riches in the bamboo for you to find."

Upon hearing this, the beautiful princess was both happy and sad. She spoke many comforting words to her parents, telling them that they must always think of her when looking at the moon. She wrote a last letter to the emperor and tucked a little phial of the Potion of Life inside, as a parting gift. Then she took her place in the chariot, and the cloud began to roll upwards

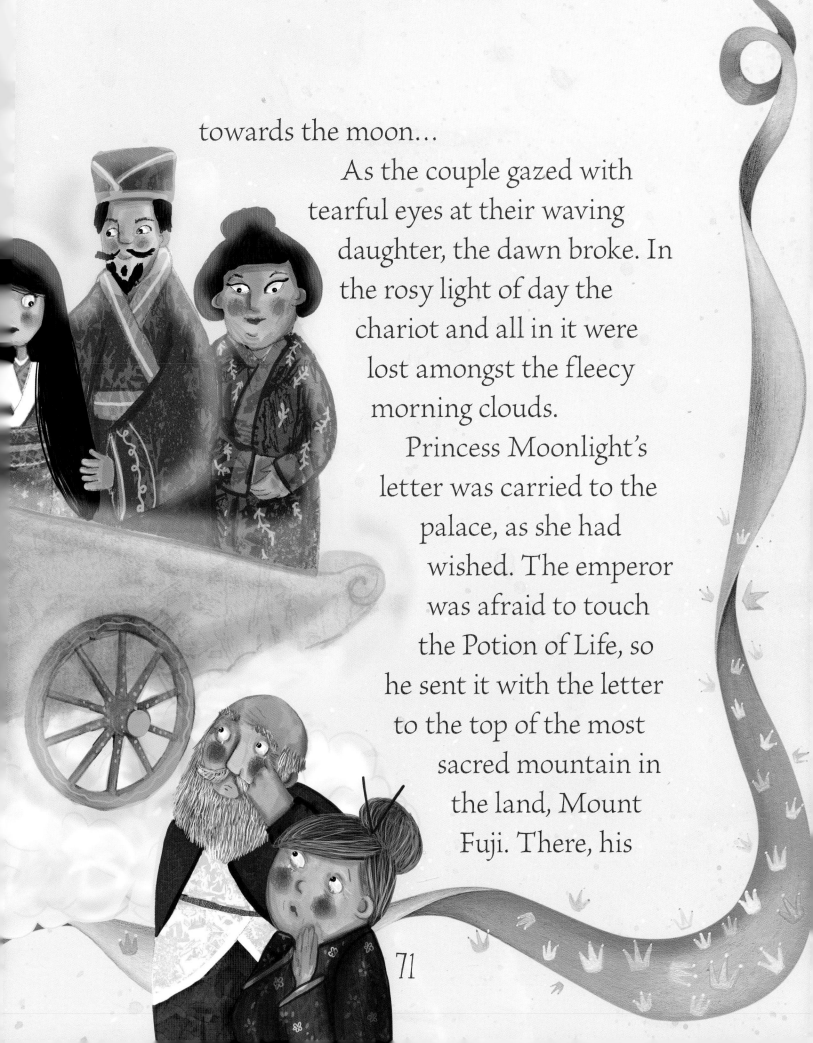

towards the moon…

As the couple gazed with tearful eyes at their waving daughter, the dawn broke. In the rosy light of day the chariot and all in it were lost amongst the fleecy morning clouds.

Princess Moonlight's letter was carried to the palace, as she had wished. The emperor was afraid to touch the Potion of Life, so he sent it with the letter to the top of the most sacred mountain in the land, Mount Fuji. There, his

71

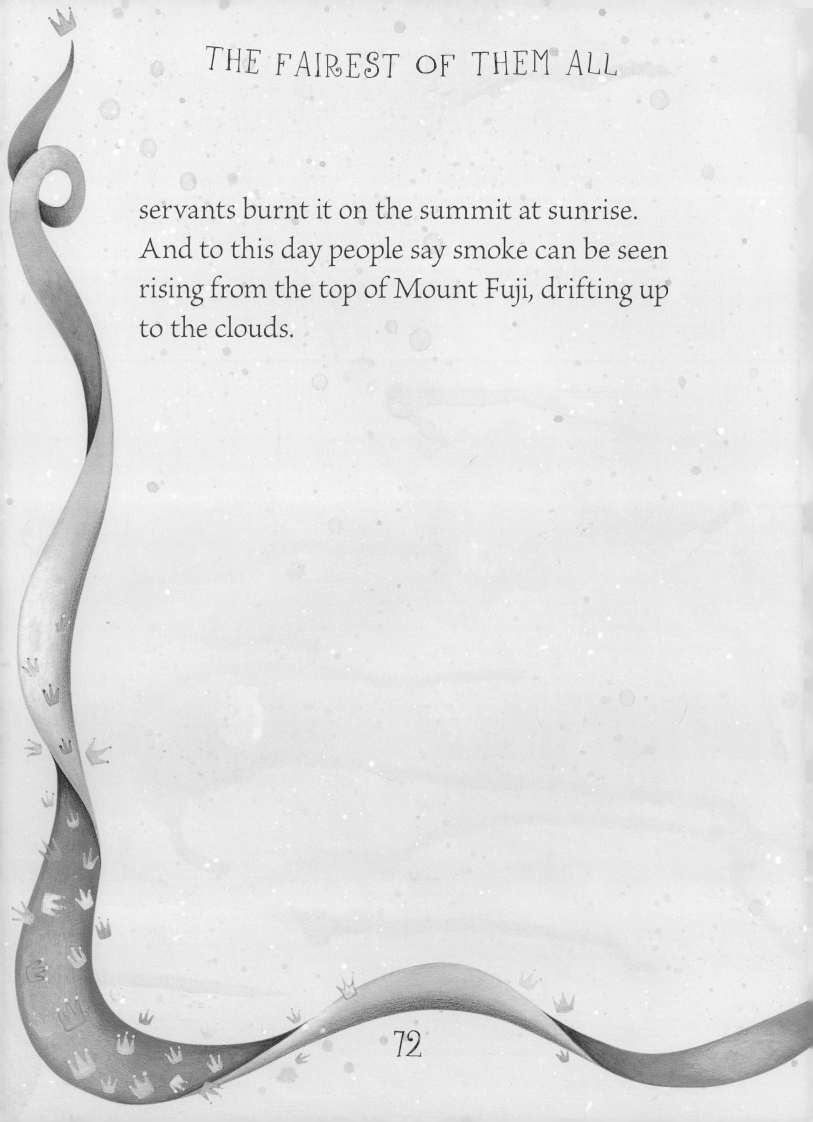

servants burnt it on the summit at sunrise. And to this day people say smoke can be seen rising from the top of Mount Fuji, drifting up to the clouds.

Princess Chatterbox

Retold from Gudrun Thorne-Thomsen's
version of a Norse fairytale

There was once a princess who was beautiful beyond compare. All other girls throughout the land were said to pale beside her. However, most unfortunately, she had a very annoying fault – she would not stop talking! She was very grumpy too, so most of her talk was arguing and moaning.

The king eventually became so tired of his beautiful daughter's non-stop quarrelling and complaining that he announced that whoever could somehow silence her would marry her – and have half of his kingdom too. There were plenty of those who wanted to try it, I can tell you, for it is not every day that you can get a beautiful princess and half a kingdom. The gate to the king's palace did not stop opening and closing for a second. Princes came in great crowds from the east and the west – and plenty of young men who weren't princes too, both riding and walking. But try as they might, not one of them could make the princess lost for words.

The beautiful princess kept on and on arguing and moaning, quarrelling and complaining, chattering and babbling... At last the king announced that those who tried and failed to silence her should have both ears marked with the red-hot branding iron with which he marked his sheep. He was certainly not going to have a constant stream of strangers in his palace and all that flurry and worry for nothing!

In a little house in the countryside, far from the palace, there lived three brothers who heard about the princess. They imagined how very beautiful she must be, and so decided to try their luck to see if they couldn't win her and half the kingdom too. The brothers were friends and good fellows, all three of them, and they set off together.

When they had walked a long way, the youngest brother – whom everyone called Boots – suddenly stopped and picked something up.

"Look what I've found!" he cried.

"What did you find?" asked his brothers.

"I found a dead crow," he said.

"Ugh! Throw it away! Whatever do you want that for?" said his brothers, who always thought they knew a great deal.

"Oh, I haven't much to carry, I might as well carry this," said Boots.

When they had walked on further, Boots again picked up something.

"I've found something else!" he cried.

"What have you found now?" said the brothers.

"I found a willow twig," he said.

"Whatever do you want with that? Throw it away!" they replied.

"Oh, I haven't much to carry, I might as well carry that," said Boots.

After the brothers had walked still further, Boots picked up something again. "Oh, lads – I've found something else!" he cried.

"Well, well. What did you find this time?" asked the brothers.

"A piece of a broken saucer," he said.

"Oh, what is the use of that? Throw it away!" they told him.

"Oh, I haven't much to carry, I might as

well carry that," said Boots.

Further along the road, Boots stooped down again and picked up something else.

"You won't believe this – I've found something else, lads!" he cried.

"And what is it now?" they asked.

"Two twisty, curly goat horns," said Boots.

"Oh! Throw them away. What could you do with them?" they said.

"Oh, I haven't much to carry, I might as well carry them," said Boots.

Yet further on down the road, he found something again.

"Oh, lads, just see what I've found this time!" he cried.

"Dear, dear, what wonderful things you do find! What is it now?" said the brothers, rolling their eyes.

"I've found a wedge of wood," he replied.

"Oh, throw it away! What do you want with that?" they said.

"Oh, I haven't much to carry, I might as well carry that," said Boots.

By now, they were nearing the king's palace. Boots picked up something once more.

"Oh, lads, see what I've found!" he cried.

"If you could only find a little common sense, it would be good for you," they said. "Well, let's see what it is now."

"A worn-out shoe sole," he replied.

"Well, that was a wonderful thing to pick up! Now throw it away! What do you want with that?" said the brothers.

"Oh, I haven't much to carry, I might as well carry that, if I am to win the princess and half the kingdom," said Boots.

"Yes, of course you are likely to do that, you foolish boy," they said.

At last they came to the king's palace. The eldest brother was first to be shown into the great hall to meet the most beautiful princess.

"Good day," he said, quite stunned by her.

"Good day to you," said the princess haughtily, "if it is a good day, which I doubt—"

"It's awfully hot in here," the brother interrupted.

"It is hotter over there in the hearth," said the princess. While she grumbled away to herself, the young man looked over at the red-hot iron, lying ready and waiting in the hearth. When he saw it, he forgot every word he was going to utter. So it was all over for him – and he left with very painful ears.

Then it was the turn of the middle brother.

"Good day," he said, marvelling at the princess's beauty.

"Good day to you," said the princess with a

sneer, "although it wasn't
such a good day for your brother—"

"It's awfully hot in here," he interrupted.

"It's hotter over there in the hearth,"
she sniffed.

When the middle brother looked at the
red-hot iron he, too, couldn't get a word out.

So they marked his ears and turned him out of the palace.

Then at last it was Boots's turn.

"Good day," he said, gazing at the most beautiful princess.

"Good day to you," she answered.

"It's nice and warm in here," Boots remarked.

"It's hotter in the hearth," she said.

"That's good, may I bake my crow there, then?" Boots fired back.

"I'm afraid it'll burst," retorted the princess, rather surprised.

"There's no danger. I'll just wind this willow twig around the bird," answered Boots, holding up the twig.

"It's too loose," the princess countered grumpily.

"Then I'll stick this wedge of wood in," said

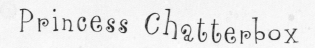

the lad, and took out the wedge.

"The fat will drop off," shot back the princess with a scowl, getting more and more annoyed.

"Then I'll hold this under," announced the lad, and pulled out the piece of broken saucer.

"You're a twisty type of young man," objected the princess, now extremely irritated indeed.

"No, I'm not twisty, but this is twisty," said the lad, and he showed her the goat's horn.

"Ooh, I've never seen anything as twisty as that!" gasped the princess, quite taken aback.

"Well, I have," said Boots, and he pulled out the other goat's horn.

"If you keep on like this, you'll wear out my very soul, you will!" the princess cried, most exasperated.

"No, I won't wear out your soul, for I have a sole that's worn out already," said the lad, and pulled out the shoe sole.

Then the princess was quite stumped. She huffed and puffed and stamped her foot... but she hadn't a word to say in reply. She had met her match.

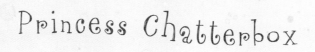

"Now, you're mine," said Boots to the most beautiful – and silent – princess with glee. And so indeed she was – and half the kingdom besides.

SEALED WITH A KISS

Sleeping Beauty

Retold from the Grimm brothers'
version of a German folk tale

A long time ago there lived a king and a queen who wished every day for a baby, but with no luck. For years they waited, longingly. Then one day, when the queen was sitting sadly by a lily pond, a little frog hopped out of the water. "Your majesty," he croaked, "this year you will have a daughter."

The startled queen did not know what to think. But indeed, later that year she gave birth to a beautiful baby girl.

The king and queen were overjoyed and threw a great feast to celebrate. They invited all their family and friends, and they also decided to ask the fairies too. There were thirteen powerful fairies in the kingdom. However, the king and queen had only twelve spaces for them in the banqueting hall. So they did not send invitations to all thirteen fairies, they left one out.

The feast was a magnificent event, which was brought to a close with a magnificent firework display. Before the delighted guests departed, the fairies came forward one by one to present the baby with magic gifts. One gave her wisdom. One gave her kindness. Another gave her beauty, and so on – everything that the princess could wish for.

However, when eleven fairies had given

their gifts, the thirteenth fairy suddenly appeared in a cloud of purple smoke! Her face was thunderous. "When the princess is eighteen," she shouted, "she will prick herself at a spinning wheel and fall down dead." Then, in a sudden flash, she vanished.

Everyone cried out in horror and despair. But then the twelfth fairy stepped forward. She still had her gift to give to the princess. "I cannot stop the curse," the fairy told the heartbroken king and queen, "but I can soften it. Your daughter will not die; she will instead fall into a deep sleep lasting a hundred years."

The very next day, the king did what he could to try to stop the dreadful curse coming true at all. He commanded that all the spinning wheels in the kingdom should be gathered up and burnt.

In the years that followed, all the gifts of

the fairies came to pass. The princess grew up so beautiful, clever, kind and modest that everyone who met her loved her.

Then came the day when the princess turned eighteen. She woke on her birthday with the sun shining and her heart full of happiness. As the princess stepped brightly through the palace on her way to join her parents for breakfast, she was struck by the sight of a narrow, winding staircase that she had never noticed before. She made her way up the steep steps and reached a little door at the top. There was a rusty key in the lock, and the princess couldn't resist turning it. With a loud creak, the door opened to reveal a little tower room in which sat an old woman at a spinning wheel.

"Good morning," said the princess, very puzzled. "Can I ask what you are doing?"

"I am spinning," said the old woman, as she sent the wheel turning.

"What is the thing that whirls round so merrily?" asked the princess, and she reached out to touch the spindle.

Ouch! It pricked her finger! And in that

92

instant, the curse was fulfilled. The thirteenth fairy – for of course, that's who the old woman really was – disappeared along with her spinning wheel. The princess sank onto a couch under the window, in a deep, dreamless sleep, which was so powerful it spread over the whole castle. The king and queen went to sleep in the dining hall, and all their courtiers with them. The horses and cows went to sleep in the fields, the dogs in the yard, the doves on the roof, and the flies on the walls. Even the flickering kitchen fire grew still, and the cook, who was pulling the kitchen boy's ear because he had burnt the porridge, fell asleep too. The wind dropped and on the trees and flowers in the castle gardens, not a leaf nor petal stirred.

Around the castle a thorny hedge began to grow – up... and up... and up... so high that at last nothing could be seen of the castle, not even the flags on the roof. The people of the kingdom were full of sorrow. They tried to chop through the hedge many times, but the branches grew back faster than they could cut, thicker and thornier than ever. So the castle remained hidden.

Many years went by, but people did not forget the lovely Briar Rose, as the princess was called. They told stories of her, which were passed down through families. From time to time bold princes came and tried to force a way through the hedge into the castle – but all returned home unsuccessful, slashed horribly by the thorns and scarred forever.

One day, a brave prince from a far-off land arrived in the kingdom. He was determined to go and look upon the lovely Briar Rose or die in the attempt. He had no idea, however, that the hundred years were at an end on that very day. It was time for Briar Rose to wake!

As the prince approached the hedge, its thick, twisted branches reached out as if to grab him… but to the prince's immense surprise, the branches suddenly shrank back, the thorns disappeared, and large, scented flowers blossomed in their place. The dense, tangled hedge before him thinned and parted into a leafy archway. The prince walked through it easily, completely unharmed, before more flowery stems sprang out and closed up the hedge behind him.

The prince found himself in the courtyard of the castle. He saw the horses, cows and dogs lying asleep. On the roof sat the doves with their heads under their wings. He went inside and saw all the people sleeping as still as statues, and the flies asleep on the walls.

Everything was so still that the prince could hear his own breathing as he passed through the corridors, searching for the princess. At last, he stumbled upon the small narrow staircase and opened the door into the little room where Briar Rose was sleeping. There she lay, looking so beautiful that the prince could not take his eyes off her. He bent down and kissed her, and at that moment, Briar Rose was woken. She opened her eyes and looked up at the prince.

Down in the dining hall, the king and queen and all the courtiers woke up too and looked at each other in astonishment. The horses and cows in the fields stood up and shook themselves. The dogs began to leap about, wagging their tails. The doves on the roof lifted their heads from under their wings, looked around, and took off into the sky.

The flies on the walls began to crawl around again. In the kitchen, the fire suddenly blazed up and the cook awoke and let go of the yawning kitchen boy's ear.

That very evening, the whole kingdom celebrated the wedding of the prince and Briar Rose, who lived happily ever after.

Little Daylight

Retold from Sara Cone Bryant's version
of a fairy story by George MacDonald

Once there was a beautiful palace which had a great wood at one side. Deep in the wood lived eight fairies. Seven of them were good fairies, who had been there always, but the eighth was a bad fairy, who had only recently arrived. The good fairies lived in the dearest little houses! One lived in a hollow silver birch, one in a little moss cottage, and so on. But the bad fairy had made her home in a horrid mud house in the middle of a dark, dank swamp.

Now when the first baby was born to the king and queen, they decided to name her 'Daylight', because she was so bright and sweet. And of course they invited the good fairies to the christening. But, alas, no one knew about the swamp fairy, so she was not invited – which really pleased her, because it gave her an excuse to do something mean.

At the christening party, five of the good fairies stepped forward, one after another, and gave little Daylight gifts. The other two were standing amongst the guests. The swamp fairy thought there were no more of them, and so she stepped forward from her hiding place.

"Here is my *gift* for little Daylight," sneered the bad fairy, "the princess shall sleep all day!" And she laughed a horrid shrieking cackle,

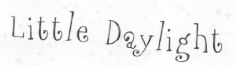

"He, he, hi, hi!", which echoed round the room. Everyone looked at everyone else in despair. But out stepped the sixth good fairy. "Then I promise that she will be able to stay awake all night," she said sadly.

"Ah!" screamed the swamp fairy. "You spoke before I had finished, which is against the rules, so I get another chance."

All the fairies started at once to say, "I beg your pardon!"

But the bad fairy continued, "I had only laughed 'he, he!' and 'hi, hi!' I still had 'ho, ho!' and 'hu, hu!' to laugh."

The fairies could not argue with this, so the bad fairy was given another chance. "Since Princess Daylight is to wake all night, she shall wax and wane with the moon! Ho, ho, hu, hu!" she cackled.

Then out stepped the seventh good fairy. "Until a prince shall kiss her without knowing who she is," she added quickly.

At this, the swamp fairy could say no more, for she had already laughed 'ho, ho!' and 'hu, hu!'

That was the end of the party, but it was only the beginning of the trouble. Little Daylight was merry and bright all night, but slept like a dormouse from dawn till dusk. Nothing could waken her while day lasted.

Still, the royal family got used to this. But the rest of the bad fairy's gift was worse. You know how the moon grows bigger and brighter each night, from a curving silver thread till it is round and golden? That is the waxing moon. Then it wanes; it grows smaller and paler again, night by night, till it disappears altogether for a while. Well, poor little Daylight waxed and waned with it. When the moon was full she was rosy, plump and merry. But when it waned, she became paler and thinner till she lay in her cradle like a shadow-baby, without sound or motion. Then with each new moon, she revived…

And so it went on as she grew up. No wonder Princess Daylight came to like being alone! She got in the habit of wandering by herself in the wood at night, playing in the moonlight when she was well. But when the moon was waning she shrank to look like a little old woman, and so she hid herself away in the shadows.

When the princess was about seventeen years old, a prince from a neighbouring country became lost in the woods while on a hunting trip. He knew nothing about Princess Daylight. He wandered about till nightfall, when he came upon a beautiful glade. It was three days from full moon, and in the bright moonlight, he saw something stir, graceful and pale. 'It must be a moon fairy,' thought the prince, and he stepped back into the shadows.

The moon fairy came nearer, dancing and

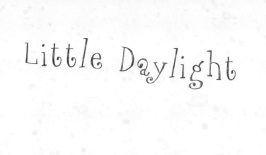

swaying in the silvery glow. And when she was quite close, the prince saw that she was not a fairy after all, but a human girl – the

loveliest he had ever seen. He could think of nothing in the world except the hope of finding out who she was and staying near her.

While he watched, enchanted, he did not notice the sky growing darker and the wind rising. Suddenly there was a loud clap of thunder. The girl danced on. But then came a great flash of lightning. The prince was blinded for a second and when his eyes cleared, he saw that the beautiful girl had fainted on the ground. The prince rushed over to help her, but she was already opening her eyes and getting to her feet.

"Who are you?" she asked.

"I'm a prince," stammered the young man. "I thought you might be hurt."

"I am Princess Daylight," smiled the girl. "Not that I know what daylight looks like," she added sadly.

"Why, doesn't everybody know that?" asked the prince, puzzled.

"I am different from everyone else," sighed the princess. "I can only wake up at night-time…" then suddenly, she realized what she was saying and grew embarrassed. She fled off through the trees – so nimbly that the prince could not keep up and he lost her. However, from that moment on, he could think of nothing but the beautiful Princess Daylight. He vowed to wander in the forest searching, until he found her.

Unfortunately, the wicked swamp fairy had seen everything in her crystal ball. She was furious, for fear that the princess should be delivered from her curse. So she cast spells to keep the prince from finding Daylight again. Night after night the poor prince wandered, and could never find the glade where he had seen the princess. And when daytime came, of course, there was no princess to be seen. Finally, at the time when the moon was almost gone, the swamp fairy stopped her spells. She knew that by this time Daylight would be so changed and ugly that the prince would never know her even if he did see her.

That night the prince did find the glade, but no princess came. He had the idea of lighting a fire, which might catch her attention if she should happen to see it. He gathered up some wood and set it blazing. Then in the glow, he suddenly caught sight of a dark heap near the foot of a big tree. Somebody was lying there!

He ran to the spot, his heart pounding with hope. But when he lifted the cloak that was huddled about the body, he saw that it

Little Daylight

was not Daylight. A pinched old woman's face looked out at him instead. Her eyes were half-closed and she was moaning faintly.

"Oh, you poor thing!" said the prince. "What is the matter?" But the old woman only moaned again. The prince lifted her and carried her over to the warm fire, and rubbed her hands, trying to revive her. Her face was so terribly strange and white that the prince's tender heart ached with pity. He leant down and kissed her withered cheek.

Suddenly, the old woman sat up and the hood fell from her face. As she looked at the prince, the first long ray of the rising sun fell upon her – it was Princess Daylight! Her hair was as golden as the sun itself and her eyes as blue as cornflowers.

The prince fell on his knees before her. But she gave him her hand and made him rise.

"You kissed me when I was an old woman," said the princess, "I'll kiss you now that I am a young princess." And she did – in the golden rays of the dawn.

The Princess and the Swineherd

Retold from a tale by Hans Christian Andersen

Once upon a time there lived quite a poor prince who only had a small kingdom. However, his name was known far and wide and there were hundreds of young women who would gladly have married him. Yet he very boldly set his sights on the emperor's daughter...

Now on the grave of the prince's father grew a rose tree, the most beautiful of its kind.

It bloomed only once in five years, and then it had only one single rose upon it – but what a rose it was! It had such a sweet scent that you instantly forgot all your troubles when you smelt it. The prince also had a nightingale which sang with the most enchanting voice ever heard. The prince decided to give the rose tree and the nightingale to the princess. Both were put into silver cases and sent to her.

The emperor ordered the gifts to be carried into the great hall where the princess was amusing herself with her ladies-in-waiting. When she saw the presents, she clapped her hands for joy. "I hope one of them is a little kitten," she said. Then the rose tree with the beautiful rose was unpacked.

"How nicely it is made," exclaimed the ladies-in-waiting.

"It is more than nice," said the emperor,

"it is truly charming."

The princess reached out to touch the petals and nearly began to cry.

"Yes, but look at it, father," she said. "It's not gold or silver and has no jewels on it at all. It's just a rose – a natural rose!"

"What a shame it is natural," repeated all her ladies.

"Let's see what the other case contains," soothed the emperor. The nightingale was taken out, singing beautifully.

"*Superbe, charmant*," said the ladies of the court, for they all prattled French, one worse than the other.

"I hope it's not just a real bird," said the princess, frowning. "Tell me that it's something really expensive."

The courtiers who had brought in the presents sighed. "Unfortunately, Your

Highness, it is a real bird," they said.

"Then let it fly away," said the princess in a huff. And she sent a message to the prince refusing to see him.

However, the prince was not discouraged. He put on common clothes and dirtied his face, and travelled to the emperor's palace. There, he knocked on the back door and asked for work.

The prince was appointed the imperial swineherd, looking after the emperor's pigs. He was given a wretchedly small room near the pigsty to live in and he worked all day long. However, he spent his evenings making a pretty pot. He put little bells all around the rim, and when the water began to boil in it, the bells played a tune. Even more wonderful, if you put your finger into the steam rising from the pot, you could at once smell what people were cooking for dinner in every house in the kingdom.

Now when the princess passed by with her ladies-in-waiting and heard the tune, she stopped to listen, delighted. "What a wonderful tune!" she cried. "Go and ask the swineherd how much the instrument is – I have to have it at once!"

So one of the ladies went to see the swineherd. "What will you take for your pot?" she asked.

"I will have ten kisses from the princess," replied the swineherd.

"God forbid," said the lady, quite horrified.

"I will not sell it for less," replied the swineherd firmly, and the lady went back to the princess.

"What did he say?" asked the princess.

"I really dare not tell you," replied the lady.

"Whisper it into my ear," ordered the princess, and the lady did so.

"That's very rude!" exclaimed the princess, and stalked off.

But when she had gone a little distance, the bells rang again so sweetly that she stopped and turned on her heel.

"Ask him," ordered the princess, "if he will be satisfied with ten kisses from one of my ladies."

"No, thank you," was the swineherd's answer. "Ten kisses from the princess, or I keep my pot."

"Oh, how annoying!" said the princess to her ladies. "Right, I'll do it! But you must all stand around me, so that nobody can see."

So the ladies-in-waiting stood in a tight circle around the princess and the swineherd. Then the princess gave the swineherd ten

kisses and she received the pot.

How she loved her new toy! The princess ordered her ladies to keep the pot boiling day and night. They knew what was cooking everywhere, from the lord chamberlain's home to the shoemaker's. The ladies danced and clapped their hands for joy.

Meanwhile the swineherd – that is to say, the prince – had made something else. It was a rattle which, when turned quickly round, played all the waltzes, gallops and polkas known since the creation of the world.

"That is *superbe*," said the princess to her ladies when they were passing by. "I simply love all those dances! Go to the swineherd and ask

118

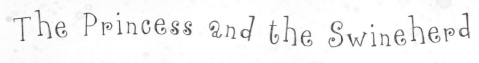

him what the instrument costs – but be sure to tell him that I shall not kiss him again." So one of the ladies-in-waiting did so, and returned with a message: "He will only sell it for a hundred kisses from the princess."

"He must be mad!" the princess cried. "I am the emperor's daughter! I should be able to have whatever I want! Tell him I will give him ten kisses, as I did the other day – the other ninety he can have from one of my ladies."

All the ladies-in-waiting gasped in horror. They were most relieved when the swineherd insisted: "A hundred kisses from the princess."

The princess gave in. "Oh, all right!" she said, stamping her foot. She ordered the ladies-in-waiting to form a tight circle around them once more. They did as they were commanded, and the princess began to kiss the swineherd.

Unfortunately, the ladies-in-waiting were so busy counting kisses that they did not notice the emperor approaching across the courtyard. He stood on tiptoe to see what was going on.

"WHAT?" he roared, when he saw his daughter kissing the swineherd. "Get out of my sight!" he bellowed, and banished both of them from his lands in disgrace.

After a long, tiring journey, the princess and the swineherd stood outside the borders of the emperor's realm, the rain pouring down on them in torrents.

"Oh, what have I done!" sobbed the princess. "If I had only been grateful for the prince's gifts and accepted his hand in marriage, none of this would have ever happened!"

Then the swineherd went behind a tree, wiped his face, and changed into the princely clothes he carried in his bag. When he stepped out again, he looked so handsome that the princess could hardly look away.

"You have no one but yourself to blame!" he

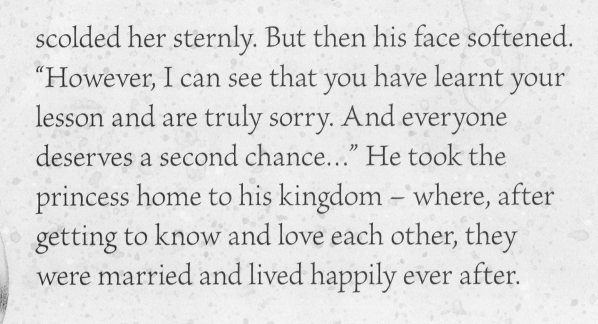

scolded her sternly. But then his face softened. "However, I can see that you have learnt your lesson and are truly sorry. And everyone deserves a second chance…" He took the princess home to his kingdom – where, after getting to know and love each other, they were married and lived happily ever after.

The Fair Fiorita

Retold from Thomas Crane's
version of an Italian fairytale

There was once an old king who had four children – three daughters and a son. The king was keen to see his daughters married before he died, so one day, he decided to have them married to the first three men who passed his palace at noon.

When noon arrived, past the palace came a swineherd, a huntsman, and a grave-digger. The king had all three summoned into his presence. He told the swineherd that he was going to marry the eldest princess, the huntsman that he would marry the middle princess, and the grave-digger that he would marry the youngest princess. At first the stunned men thought they were dreaming, but when they realized the king was serious, they were very pleased.

The prince loved his sisters dearly and was grief-stricken at their fate. He begged his father to change his mind, but the king would not listen. The prince was so upset that he could not bring himself to attend the princesses' wedding. Instead, he went for a walk in the garden. While he was doing so, to his astonishment, the garden suddenly bloomed with the fairest flowers. Out of a cloud came a voice, which boomed: "Happy is he who shall have a kiss from the lips of the

fair Fiorita!" At this, the prince decided that
he would wander the world until he found the
fair Fiorita and kissed her, so he could be
happy once more.

He travelled over land and sea, over
mountains and plains, but found no one that
could give him word of the fair Fiorita.
However, after three years, he arrived one day
at a palace. He stopped to drink at a fountain
there, and a young woman ran out to meet
him. She hugged and kissed him, crying:
"Welcome, welcome, my brother!"

Then the prince recognized her to be his
eldest sister! He embraced her in turn,
exclaiming, "How glad I am to see you!" And
they rejoiced greatly.

His sister took him to meet her husband,
who welcomed the prince just as warmly. The
prince asked about his other two sisters, and

his brother-in-law replied that they were well and living happily with their husbands. The prince was most surprised to hear that all three men had been enchanted by a magician, and so had become wealthy nobles.

"I must go and see them," the prince declared eagerly.

His sister told him the way and her husband – the former swineherd – gave him a gift of some hog's bristles, saying, "If you find yourself in danger, throw them on the ground."

The prince thanked him and set off to see his second sister. She too was living happily in a grand palace and welcomed him with great joy. When his visit was done, she gave him directions to his youngest sister. Her husband – the former huntsman – handed him a gift of a bunch of birds' feathers, telling him, "If you find yourself in danger, throw them on the ground."

The prince thanked him most sincerely and set off to see his youngest sister. She received him with the warmest welcome of all, for they had always loved each other the best. To the prince's delight, his sister told him that the fair Fiorita – who was a king's daughter – lived only a day's journey away! Her husband – the former grave-digger – gave the prince a present of a little human bone, saying, "If you find yourself in danger, throw this on the ground."

The prince thanked him most sincerely and set off at once for the fair Fiorita's kingdom. There, he heard talk that the king set impossible tasks for any man who came seeking the hand of the princess in marriage – and had each suitor put to death when he failed! The prince knew he had to think up a clever plan.

It was well known that the king liked to buy for his daughter the rarest musical instruments. So the prince went to a music-box maker and told him, "I want an amazing music-box that will play three tunes – each tune to last a day. Make it in such a way that a person can hide inside it."

When the music-box was ready, the prince hid himself inside and had it delivered to the king's palace. It was thought to be so astonishing that it was carried straight to Princess Fiorita in her chamber – and she was delighted with it too!

That night, when the palace was silent and still, the prince climbed out of the music-box. He gazed at the sleeping princess – she was the most beautiful girl he had ever seen and he

fell in love with her at once. He whispered, "Fair Fiorita! Fair Fiorita!" and she woke up in a fright. But the prince

had such a kind face and spoke to her so sweetly that she soon forgot her fear and fell quite in love with him, too.

When the first rays of dawn began to lighten the chamber, the prince said, "Fair Fiorita, give me, I beg you, a kiss. If you do not, I shall die."

129

Blushing, the princess shyly gave him a kiss – and on the prince's lips there remained a beautiful rose. He took the rose, climbed out of the window, and slipped away from the palace before he was discovered.

The prince was completely in love, and so later that same day, he presented himself to the king and asked for the fair Fiorita's hand in marriage. The king agreed – if the prince could complete four tasks...

For the first task, the king shut the prince up in a large room full of fruit. He commanded him, on pain of death, to eat it all up in one day. The prince was at first in despair, but then he remembered the hog's bristles and threw them down on the ground. Suddenly there appeared a great herd of swine which ate up all the fruit, and then disappeared. The task was accomplished!

So the king proposed another. He told the prince to make him fall asleep! The prince had no idea how to do this – but then he remembered the bunch of feathers and threw them down on the ground. At once there appeared the loveliest bird in the world, which sang such a sweet lullaby that the king's head drooped and he began to doze. The second task was accomplished!

So the king set the third task. "You must present me with a child who is just two years old, but who can speak and call me by name," he demanded. The prince was stumped – but then he remembered the little bone and threw it down on the ground. At once, a beautiful little child ran into the throne room, and bowed to the king and greeted him by name most graciously.

"Bravo!" said the king. "But unless you

succeed in the final task, you will surely die. I have hidden my daughter away with a group of other maidens, all dressed the same and with their faces covered by veils. You must find the hiding place and then guess which is Princess Fiorita."

The prince's heart gladdened. He took out the rose from the princess's kiss and it led him through the twisting, turning corridors of the palace, straight to the room in which the young ladies were hidden. When the prince opened the door, the rose pointed directly to Princess Fiorita!

Astonished, the king gave the pair his blessing. Taking the crown from his head, he put it on the prince's. "This is now yours," he declared. A few days later, a splendid wedding feast was held, to which the prince's three sisters and their husbands were invited. Even

the prince's father came – and he gave his son his crown too. So the prince and the fair Fiorita became king and queen of two realms, and from that time on were always happy.

The Princess and the Frog

Retold from the Grimm brothers'
version of a German folk tale

A long time ago, when wishes could still come true, there lived a king with three grown-up daughters. Close by the castle lay a great, dark forest in which there was a well. Whenever the day was very warm, the king's youngest daughter went out into the cool shade of the forest and sat down at the side of the well. There, she would take out her favourite golden ball and throw and catch it, to while away the time.

It so happened that on one occasion the princess's golden ball slipped through her outstretched fingers and landed – *splosh!* – in the well. The dismayed princess thought her ball had sunk and was gone forever, and she began to cry. She sobbed and sobbed – until suddenly she heard someone say, "What's the matter, princess?"

She looked all about. There was no one there except a big, slimy frog sitting on the edge of the well, peering up at her with bulbous eyes.

"Is that you, frog?" the princess wondered aloud. "I am weeping for my favourite golden ball, which has fallen into the well," she explained, looking curiously at the frog.

"There, there – don't cry," soothed the frog. "I can bring your ball back. But what will you give me in thanks?"

The excited princess thought quickly. "Whatever you want, dear frog!" she promised. "My clothes… my pearls and jewels… you can even have the golden crown I am wearing."

The frog gulped and answered, "I do not care for such things. All I want is for you to be my friend. I would like to keep you company and play with you. To sit next you at mealtimes, and eat off your little golden plate and drink out of your little golden cup. To snuggle up to you at night-time in your little bed… If you promise me this now, I will dive down into the well and fetch your golden ball."

The princess replied without any hesitation: "Oh, yes! I promise!"

At this, the frog grinned broadly. He leapt

straight into the murky green water and vanished. In a short time, he came swimming up again with the ball in his mouth, which he threw onto the grass.

The king's daughter scooped up her precious ball and ran away with it delightedly.

"Wait, wait!" croaked the frog. "Take me with you! I can't run like you can!"

But the princess took no notice – she just hurried home. The poor frog had to slink back to his gloomy well. By nightfall, the princess had forgotten all about him. And she didn't give him a thought all the next day either.

When evening came, the princess seated herself in the great hall with her father, sisters and all the courtiers, as usual. She was eating from her little golden plate when something came creeping – *splish, splash, splish, splash* – up the marble staircase. When it reached

the top, it knocked on the door and cried, "Youngest princess! Open the door for me."

The princess ran straight away to see who it was. Imagine her horror when she opened the door and there sat the frog. Hastily, she slammed the door to and took her seat at the table again.

The king saw plainly that she was very shaken. "My child, whatever are you so afraid of?" he asked.

"A frog, father," the princess replied, very pale. "It's a disgusting frog."

"A frog?" guffawed the king. "Whatever does he want with you?"

So the princess explained what had happened. "I never thought he would follow me to the castle!" she protested.

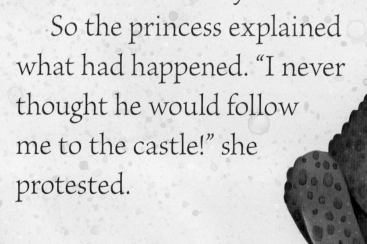

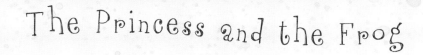

Just then, the frog knocked a second time, and cried, "Youngest princess! Open the door!" The king looked very sternly at his youngest daughter. "You must keep your promise," he told her. "Go and let him in."

Reluctantly, the princess did as she was told. The frog hopped in at her feet and followed her to her chair. He sat squatly on the floor and croaked, "Lift me up."

The king ordered the princess to do what he asked.

Once the frog was on the chair, he wanted to be on the table. And when he was on the table he said, "Now, push your little golden plate nearer to me so that we may eat together." The princess did this, but it was clear that she didn't want to at all. The frog greatly enjoyed what he ate, but the princess could barely manage a mouthful.

At length, the frog said, "What a lovely meal! I am all full up. Now I am tired, carry me up to your bedroom and let's go to sleep."

The princess pulled a face, for she did not want to touch the frog – let alone have him sleep next to her in her pretty little bed. "You should be kind to the creature who helped you!" the king exclaimed angrily.

So the princess took hold of the frog with two fingers, wrinkling her nose. She carried him upstairs and put him in the darkest corner of her room. The princess jumped into bed and drew the covers up under her chin. But the frog crept over to her. "I am tired," he said, "and I want to sleep in your comfy bed. Lift me up with you, or I will tell your father!"

The Princess and the Frog

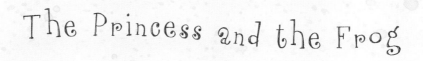

The princess shuddered, but did what she was told. Yet the worst was to come.

"You have forgotten something," croaked the frog. "Before I settle down, you should kiss me goodnight."

Horrified, the princess stifled a sob. She shut her eyes, pursed her mouth, and bent

towards the slimy creature in her bed. But the second her lips touched his lumpy, clammy skin, she could not help giving a little cry of disgust and sweeping him away from her, off onto the floor.

She opened her eyes and, to her astonishment, the frog was nowhere to be seen. Instead, standing in front of her was a handsome young man. He had a kind, gentle face and fell to one knee before her, speaking softly so she would not be afraid.

He explained that he was a prince, who had been bewitched and turned into a frog by a wicked fairy. The princess's kiss had broken the curse and set him free!

The prince was so kind and handsome that the princess fell in love with him at once. When they went and told the king what had happened, he was delighted. So the very next

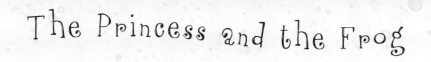

day, the couple rode away to the prince's kingdom, where they were greeted with much rejoicing.

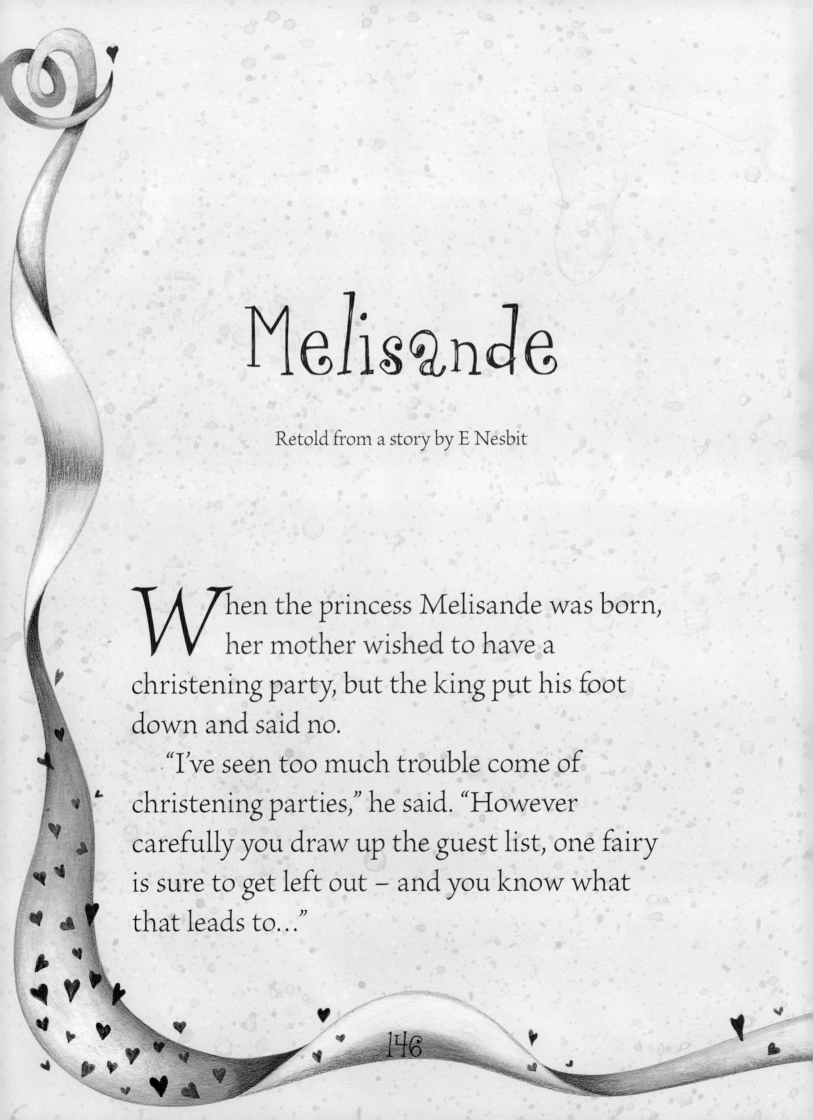

Melisande

Retold from a story by E Nesbit

When the princess Melisande was born, her mother wished to have a christening party, but the king put his foot down and said no.

"I've seen too much trouble come of christening parties," he said. "However carefully you draw up the guest list, one fairy is sure to get left out – and you know what that leads to…"

"Perhaps you're right," sighed the queen. "My cousin forgot a stuffy old fairy when she was sending out the invitations for her daughter's christening. The old wretch turned up at the last moment and the girl drops toads out of her mouth to this day."

"Just so," said the king. "We won't ask a single fairy to the christening – then none of them can be offended."

"Unless they all are," said the queen.

And that was exactly what happened. When the king and the queen and the baby got back from the christening, the butler met them at the door, looking flustered. "Please, Your Majesties, there are seven hundred very angry fairies waiting for you in the Throne Room," he told them hurriedly.

With a sigh, the queen opened the door and began: "I'm very sorry—"

"Hold your tongue," interrupted the most wicked fairy, Malevola, very rudely. "Don't make excuses," she said. "You know what happens if a fairy is left out of a christening party. We are all going to give our presents now. I will begin: the princess shall be bald."

The queen nearly fainted as Malevola drew back and another fairy in a smart black bonnet with snakes on it stepped forward, ready to curse the baby too. But the king held up his hand firmly.

"Oh no you don't!" he said. "Have none of you ladies been to fairy school? Surely you know that a fairy who breaks the traditions of fairy history goes out like the flame of a candle. And tradition shows that only one bad fairy ever casts a spell at a christening party. So Malevola has spoken and that's it – no one else! Do I make myself clear?"

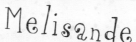

Melisande

Several of the older fairies began to murmur that actually the king was right.

"Try it, if you don't believe me," said the king. "Who's going to risk it first?"

No one answered, and the fairies began to slink quietly out of the door.

When the very last fairy had gone, the queen ran to look at her baby. She tore off her little cap and fought to hold back the tears at the sight. For all the baby's downy golden hair came off with the cap, and Princess Melisande was as bald as an egg.

"It's ok, my love," said the king. "I have a wish lying by, which I've never had occasion to use. My fairy godmother gave it to me for a wedding present, but since then I've had nothing to wish for!"

"Thank you, dear," said the queen, smiling in spite of herself.

"I'll keep the wish till the baby grows up," the king went on. "Then I'll give it to her, and if she would like to wish for hair she can."

So Princess Melisande grew up as beautiful as the sunshine and as good as gold, but never a hair grew on her head. And on the day of her eighteenth birthday, the king unlocked his gold safe, took out the wish and gave it to his daughter.

Melisande thought for a moment, and then came up with a suitable wish. "Father, I wish that all your subjects should be quite happy."

But they were that already, because the king and queen were so good. So the wish still remained.

Then Melisande said, "I wish them all to be good." But they were that already, because they were happy. So again the wish hung fire.

"Dearest, for my sake, wish what I tell you," said the queen, and she whispered in Melisande's ear.

Then Melisande said aloud, "I wish I had golden hair a yard long, and that it would grow an inch every day and grow twice as fast every time it was cut, until it was so long it weighed as much as me—"

"Stop!" cried the king in alarm. But the wish had come true, and the very next moment the princess stood smiling at him through a shower of golden hair.

"What's the matter dear?" the queen asked.

"You'll find out soon enough," answered the king.

And indeed, they did. The princess's hair began by being a yard long, and it grew an inch every night. In about five weeks her hair was about two yards long. It trailed on the floor and swept up all the dust. And still the princess's hair was growing an inch every night. When it was three yards long it was so heavy that Melisande could not bear it any longer. So she took

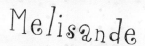

some scissors and cut it all off, and for a few hours she was comfortable. But the hair went on growing... and now it grew twice as fast as before, so that in thirty-six days it was as long as ever.

The poor princess cried with tiredness. When she couldn't bear it any more she cut her hair and was comfortable for a very short time. For the hair now grew four times as fast as at first. In eighteen days it was as long as before, and she had to have it cut again. Then it grew eight inches a day. And after the next cut it grew sixteen inches a day. And so on, growing twice as fast after each cut, until the princess went to bed at night with her hair clipped short and woke up in the morning

with golden hair flowing all about the room. The royal hairdresser had to come and cut all the hair off before she could get out of bed.

"Oh I wish I was bald again," sighed poor Melisande often.

One day, the king came across her weeping bitterly. "I shall write to my fairy godmother," he said to the queen, "and see if something cannot be done."

So he wrote and sent the letter by a skylark, and in return came this answer: "Why not advertise for a competent prince? Offer the usual reward."

The king sent out his heralds all over the world to proclaim that any respectable prince could marry Princess Melisande if he could somehow stop her hair growing. From far and near came hordes of princes anxious to try their luck. They brought all sorts of nasty

remedies with them in bottles and jars and boxes, but none of them worked – and Melisande was glad, for she didn't like any of the princes.

Melisande now had to sleep in the great Throne Room, as it was the only room big enough to contain all her hair. One night, she was sitting at the window when she saw a new arrival walking in the garden in the moonlight. For the first time, she found herself wishing that a prince might actually have the power to stop her hair from growing.

The prince looked up and said, "You are Princess Melisande? I am Prince Florizel. There is a sturdy-looking tree just below your window – may I climb up to you?"

"Surely," said the princess. So he climbed up to the window.

"Now," he said, smiling kindly, "if I can do what your father asks, would you want to marry me?"

"Oh yes," she replied.

"I need a kiss to seal the promise," he said.

And the princess gladly gave him a kiss, and then another (so as not to be thought mean) and one more – just for luck.

The next day, the prince ordered for a pair of giant gold weighing scales to be made. When they were ready, he had them put out in the palace gardens under the branches of a big oak tree.

"Do you trust me?" he asked Princess Melisande, taking her hand.

"Of course I do," she replied. Then Florizel took her down into the garden and helped her up to sit in one side of the scale.

"What is going into the other scale?" asked Melisande.

"Your hair," said Florizel. "You see, your hair has not been able to tell when it's the same weight as you. So, if we measure it, and snip it off at exactly the right weight, it should not go on growing any more…"

So when Melisande was ready, Prince Florizel swung his sword and cut off the princess's hair, and at once it began to grow at a frightful rate. The king and queen busily packed the hair into the other scale as it grew, and gradually the scale began to go down. The prince stood waiting between the scales with his sword drawn, and just before the two were equal he struck. In the seconds it took his sword to flash through the air Melisande's hair grew still more, so at the very moment when his sword struck the scales were in perfect balance.

The scale full of golden hair bumped down onto the ground. Prince Florizel hurried to help Melisande out of the other scale. And at last, the princess stood there before those who loved her, both laughing and crying with happiness, because her hair was finally quite short and not growing any more! She kissed her handsome Prince Florizel a hundred times, and the very next day they were married in a joyful celebration with a great feast and lots of dancing. And of course, every single fairy in the kingdom was invited!

DAMSELS IN DISTRESS

Andromeda and the Sea Monster

Retold from Hamilton, Wright and Mabie's
version of an ancient Greek myth

Perseus was a hero truly favoured by the
gods. His sword had been given to him by
his father, the great god Zeus, who ruled over
all the other gods and goddesses of Mount
Olympus. Zeus had also given Perseus a
Helmet of Darkness which made him
invisible. His burnished shield had been given
to him by the wise goddess Athena. And the
messenger of the gods, Hermes, had given him

winged sandals, so he could speed through the air as fast as the wind. With the help of these gifts, Perseus had slain Medusa the Gorgon, a monstrous woman with snakes for hair. She was so terrifying that anyone who saw her had turned to stone! However, the brave Perseus had used the reflection in his shield to look upon her and had slashed her head from her neck. Now Perseus was flying back to his homeland of Greece, to visit Mount Olympus and take the gods a gift – Medusa's head!

The hero soared towards the north-east, over many a league of sea, until he came to the rolling sand hills of the shore. Then he raced far across the desert and over treacherous mountains until he came to the craggy cliffs where another ocean began. He peered downwards and there, at the water's edge, he saw a white image under a dark rock.

'This,' he thought, 'must surely be the statue of some god. I will go near and see who it is that the people here worship.'

But when he drew close, he saw that it was not a statue at all. It was a living, breathing young woman! He could see her golden hair streaming in the breeze and noticed how she shrank and shivered when the waves drenched her with freezing salt spray.

The maiden's arms were raised over her head, chained to the rock. Her head hung down – she seemed exhausted and filled with grief. Every now and then she looked up and wailed and called for her mother. But she did not see Perseus, for the Helmet of Darkness was upon his head.

The hero was full of outrage and pity, and he drew even nearer. Lifting the helmet from his head, he flashed into view. The young woman cried out with terror, but Perseus spoke gently to calm her. "Don't be afraid – I will not harm you! What cruel people have bound you up here? I will set you free."

He drew his mighty sword and at once hacked through the chains as easily as if they were silk.

"Now," Perseus said, "tell me what happened to you. Why are you here?"

And she answered, weeping: "I am Princess Andromeda, the daughter of King Cepheus of Iopa. My mother is Queen Cassiopoeia. I was bound up here because she made a terrible mistake. She once boasted aloud that I was more beautiful than any mermaid who lives in the sea. The ocean god, Poseidon, heard her and was furious. He sent a terrible sea monster to come and terrorize our lands. The monster comes ashore every so often and devours any living thing he finds; animals, men, women – even children, he has no mercy. My parents prayed to the gods to tell them what they could do to stop the beast. The priests told them that the only thing which will put an end to our kingdom's suffering is if I am sacrificed – if the sea monster devours me!"

But Perseus just smiled kindly. "A sea monster?" he said. "I have fought with much worse. I will face any beast the gods care to send, for your sake, princess!"

Andromeda looked up at the hero standing there so boldly with his shield in one hand and in the other his glittering sword, and new hope lit up in her breast. But then the princess looked out to sea and saw the white foam of a mighty wave rolling in. She knew that the swell marked the arrival of the monster, rushing forwards through the deep. "There he comes, as they promised!" she cried. "Now it is my time to die! How will I bear it? Oh, go! Go quickly to safety!" And she tried to thrust Perseus away.

Yet the hero stood firm. "I will go – but only if you promise me one thing. If I slay this beast you will be my wife and come back with me to my kingdom. Promise me, and seal it with a kiss."

The princess lifted her face and kissed him. Then Perseus let out a joyful laugh and flew upwards, while Andromeda crouched, trembling, on the rock.

The immense head and shoulders of the great sea monster at last broke the surface. On he came, powering along like a dark, hulking ship. His sides were fringed with shells and seaweed, and water gurgled in and out of his great jaws. His wake foamed white behind him and before him the fish fled, leaping urgently. At last he saw Andromeda and let out a roar of hunger. He shot forward to snatch his prey.

Then, from high in the air, down swooped Perseus like a shooting star. Andromeda hid her face in terror as he shouted his warrior cry. She heard the roaring of the beast as Perseus attacked… a mighty howl split the skies… and then there was silence except for the crashing of the waves.

At last, Andromeda dared to look up. She could see no sign of the monster, only a seething mass of white bubbles where the slain beast had sunk to the bottom.

The triumphant Perseus then leapt back to the rock, lifted Andromeda into his arms and flew up with her, over the cliffs and away to the city.

In the palace, the grief-stricken king and queen sat in sackcloth and ashes on the floor of their great hall. They were sobbing as they waited to hear the news that their daughter had been killed by the monster. Imagine their astonishment and joy when Princess Andromeda ran to them, alive and well! They could not believe their eyes – it was as if she had come back to them from the dead!

The overwhelmed king and queen did not know how to thank Perseus. "Mighty hero," said King Cepheus, "you must stay here with us – I will give you my daughter's hand in marriage and half of my kingdom!"

"I will joyfully marry Princess Andromeda," Perseus replied. "But although I thank you most sincerely for the offer of half your kingdom, I will not take it. I long for my homeland of Greece and must return to my parents, who are waiting for me."

"Please just remain with us for a year," Cepheus implored him. "Our daughter has been returned to us as though from the dead – you must not take her away so soon."

So Perseus agreed, and a magnificent wedding feast was held, which lasted for seven days and nights. As the year came to an end, Perseus ordered a noble ship to be built, more elegant than any ship ever seen in those parts before. When it was ready, he had the ship loaded with treasures such as rare cloths and spices from the east, as well as plenty of gold and jewels. At long last, he and Andromeda sailed away.

But their story was never forgotten. Perseus and Andromeda had four sons and three daughters, and died at a good old age. And when they died, the goddess Athena brought them up into the heavens to join King Cepheus and Queen Cassiopoeia. If you look up on starlit nights you may see them shining there still – Cepheus with his kingly crown, Cassiopoeia plaiting her star-spangled tresses, and Perseus holding the Gorgon's head. You may also see fair Andromeda beside him, her long white arms spread out across the heavens, as she stood when chained to the rock in the rough waves, waiting to be devoured by the terrifying sea monster. All night long they

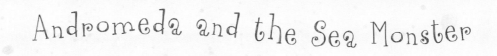

shine, a beacon to guide wandering sailors. And all day they feast with the gods, on the still blue peaks of Mount Olympus.

The Princess and the Pea

Retold from a story by Hans Christian Andersen

Once upon a time, in a land far away, there was a prince who wanted to marry a princess – but she had to be a *real* princess. The prince wasn't sure exactly what a real princess would be like, but he knew he would recognize one when he met her.

The prince travelled all over the world, but he couldn't find the kind of girl he was looking for anywhere. He met many kings' daughters, in countries near and far. Some were kind, and others were mean. Some were interesting, others were dull. Some were beautiful, others were plain. Some were clever, others were silly. Some were fun to be with, others were downright hard work. But the prince always found that, whatever they were like, the young ladies did not seem to him to be real princesses. There was always something about them that wasn't quite right. So after many months and thousands of miles of searching, the prince came home again. He was very sad, for he would have liked very much to have a real princess to love.

One evening, the prince was sitting in the great hall of the castle with his parents, mulling over what a real princess might be like, when a terrible storm came on. Thunder crashed overhead, rolling from side to side

175

across the skies. Blinding flashes of lightning lit up the windows, and torrents of rain came plunging down over the turrets in waterfalls.

Through all the din of the storm, the prince suddenly thought he heard a knocking at the castle door. He listened very carefully... yes, there it was again – it was definitely someone knocking. But who would possibly be out on such a terrible night? The prince sent a servant at once to go and see.

When the servant heaved open the big castle door, he couldn't believe his eyes. Standing there, all on her own, was a young woman. And good gracious, what a sight the rain and the wind had made her look! The water streamed from her soaked hair and drenched clothes – it poured into the toes of her shoes and out again at the heels.

The servant hurried the poor young

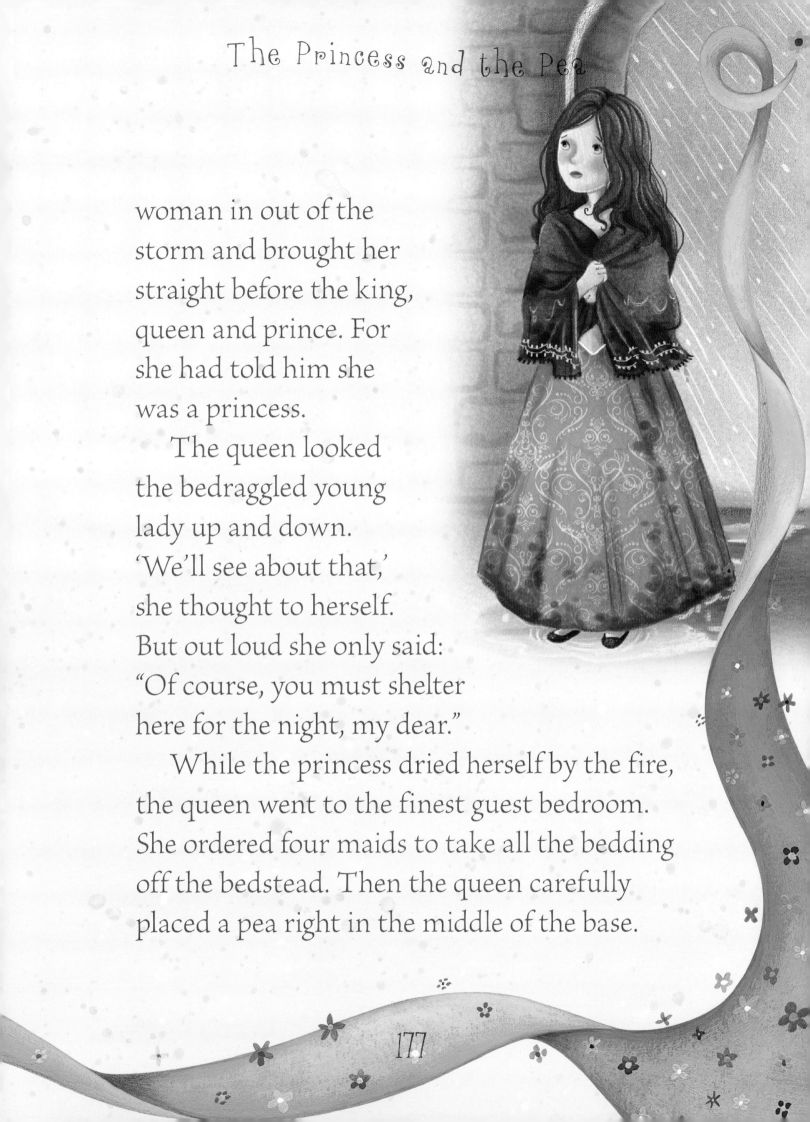

woman in out of the
storm and brought her
straight before the king,
queen and prince. For
she had told him she
was a princess.

The queen looked
the bedraggled young
lady up and down.
'We'll see about that,'
she thought to herself.
But out loud she only said:
"Of course, you must shelter
here for the night, my dear."

While the princess dried herself by the fire,
the queen went to the finest guest bedroom.
She ordered four maids to take all the bedding
off the bedstead. Then the queen carefully
placed a pea right in the middle of the base.

Next, she ordered the maids to pile twenty mattresses on top of the pea, then to lie twenty feather quilts on top of the mattresses.

This was the bed that the princess had to lie on all night.

First thing in the morning, the queen told her husband and son what she had done. And when the princess came down to breakfast, the queen asked her straight away how she had slept.

"Oh, very badly!" the poor girl sighed. "I have scarcely closed my eyes all night. Heaven only knows what was in the bed, but I was lying on something so hard that I've got bruises all over! It was horrible!"

The prince's eyes opened wide in surprise. She was a real princess – she had to be! She had felt the pea right through the twenty mattresses and the twenty feather quilts –

only a real princess could possibly be as sensitive as that.

The prince was overjoyed, for he knew that he had at last found a real princess.

It wasn't long before a magnificent wedding was held for the couple, with celebrations for all the people which went on, day and night, for an entire week. As for the pea, it was put into a museum – where it may still be seen, if no one has stolen it. For of course, this is a true story.

The Princess who was Hidden Underground

Retold from Andrew Lang's version of a German folk tale

There was once a king who had a daughter whom he loved very much. She grew up to be very beautiful, and princes and noblemen from many kingdoms began to ask for her hand in marriage. But the king did not want his daughter to get married and leave him, so he decided to set the suitors an impossible task. That way, he would not have to offend anyone by saying they couldn't marry his daughter, and neither would he have to agree to giving anyone her hand in marriage. The king hoped that in this way, he could keep the princess at home with him forever.

So the king ordered a splendid palace to be built underground. He swore the architect and all the labourers to secrecy – and when the palace was finally finished, he gave a sudden order that they were all to be killed! Now the king was the only person in the world who knew where the underground palace was – in fact, he was the only person in the world who knew that an underground palace existed at all!

Next, to the princess's horror, he locked her up inside. The king then sent out heralds all over the world with a proclamation: whoever could find his daughter could marry her.

However, anyone who tried and failed would be immediately put to death.

Of course, young men from far and wide began flocking to the palace to attempt to seek the princess. They hunted high and low until they were exhausted – but eventually, all of them met a nasty end. Still, it did not put others off from trying. Each new day brought a fresh queue of young men lining up at the palace gates.

One day, in a distant part of the kingdom, a very clever and handsome young man made up his mind that he would try to win the princess – or die in the attempt. He thought and thought, and thought a bit more, and finally came up with a plan he believed might work...

First, the young man went to see a friend of his, who was a shepherd. He knew that this

shepherd owned an extraordinary golden
fleece. He begged the shepherd to sew him
into the fleece, so he looked like a golden
sheep. At last the shepherd agreed and then
took him, disguised this way, to see the king.
The king was utterly taken in by the

magical-looking creature. He asked the shepherd to sell him the golden sheep.

As the young man had instructed, the shepherd answered: "No, Your Majesty, I will not sell my amazing sheep. However, as you like it so much, I am willing to lend it to you for three days. There's no charge, but after the three days you must give it back to me."

The king was most pleased and agreed very readily to this arrangement. So the shepherd left his 'prize sheep' with the delighted king and went away.

As the young man had thought, the king at once made ready to take the sheep to his daughter. He put a golden rope around the sheep's neck and led it through a secret entrance and down hidden passageways to the underground palace.

The king led the sheep through many

rooms until he came to a locked door. He shouted, "Open, Sartara Martara of the earth!" and the door swung open.

After that they went through many more rooms until they arrived at another locked door. Again the king called out, "Open, Sartara Martara of the earth!" and this door opened like the other.

Finally, they entered the rooms where the princess lived. Of course, she was amazed and totally charmed by the sheep! She stroked it and played with it and was greatly cheered up by it. After a while the golden rope came off of the sheep's neck, so the creature was wandering free. "Look, father, shouldn't we tie him up again?" the princess said.

"It's only a sheep – why shouldn't it roam about free?" the king replied.

Then the time came when he had to return

above ground. So he said goodbye to the princess and left the sheep with her for two days to keep her company.

Once night had fallen, the young man threw off the sheepskin. He approached the princess's bed and woke her gently. She was afraid at first, but he explained who he was. "Why ever did you come here disguised like that?" she asked him.

"I knew I had to think of some clever trick to find you, if I was to win your hand in marriage!" the young man answered.

The princess was very pleased. "You have done very well so far," she told him, "but you haven't won me quite yet. Here's what my father will do next. He will change me and my ladies-in-waiting into ducks. Then he will ask you, 'Which is the princess?' But when he says this, look at us all very carefully. I will turn my head and start to clean my wings with my bill, so you can tell which duck is me."

The princess and the young man spent a delightful two days chatting and getting to know one another, by which time they had fallen deeply in love. Early on the third day, the princess helped the handsome young man to conceal himself inside the sheepskin once more. Not long afterwards, the king arrived and took the sheep back to his own palace, where the shepherd was waiting for it.

The very next day, a young man strode up to the gates of the palace, whistling merrily. "Your Highness, I think I can find your daughter," he told the king, quite confidently.

The king was impressed by this bold new arrival, so he said, "My son, I beg you not to try. Many young men who have tried and failed have been put to death – I don't want to see you meet the same end."

But the young man answered, "I accept your conditions, Your Highness. I will either find her or lose my head."

"Then so be it," sighed the king.

However, the king's pity soon changed to astonishment. The young man led him straight to the secret entrance and down the hidden passages. When they came to the great door, the young man stopped and looked at the king. "Say the words which command it to open," he told him.

The king pretended not to know what the young man was talking about. "Whatever do you mean?" he answered.

"Call out, 'Open, Sartara Martara of the earth,'" the young man said.

So the king spoke the words, the door swung open, and he was left gnawing his

moustache in anger.

When they came to the second door, the same thing happened as at the first, and they went in and found the princess.

The king was furious, but was forced to admit defeat. "Yes, you have managed to find the princess," he said. "But now I am going to turn her and all her ladies-in-waiting into ducks. If you can guess which of these ducks is my daughter, then you shall have her for your wife."

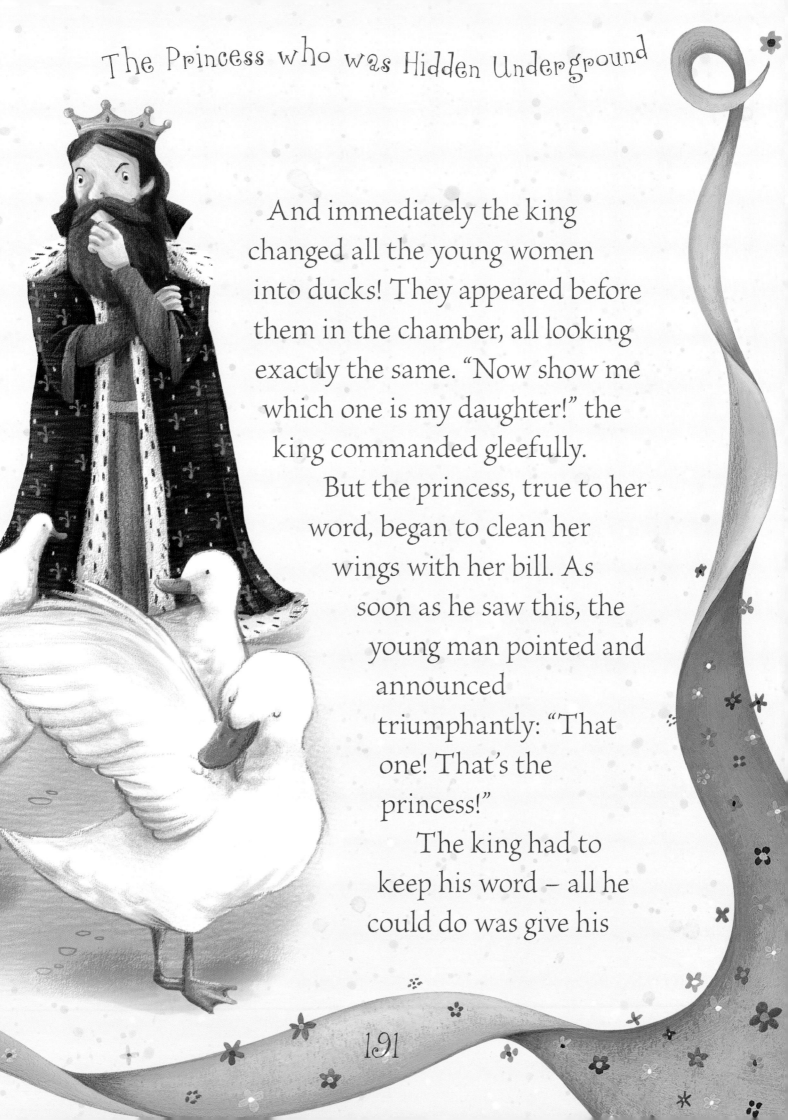

And immediately the king changed all the young women into ducks! They appeared before them in the chamber, all looking exactly the same. "Now show me which one is my daughter!" the king commanded gleefully.

But the princess, true to her word, began to clean her wings with her bill. As soon as he saw this, the young man pointed and announced triumphantly: "That one! That's the princess!"

The king had to keep his word – all he could do was give his blessing to the couple. The princess and the young man were married amid much rejoicing, and they lived together in happiness for the rest of their lives.

The Princess who was Stolen

Retold from the *Ramayana* by the poet Valmiki

Long, long ago in India, there lived a princess called Sita, who was said to be the most beautiful, gracious woman in all the world – so beautiful and gracious that some said she was in fact a goddess. Sita was the wife of Prince Rama, the son of a great king. He was a bold and mighty warrior, and was expected to become a great king himself one day. However, his stepmother was very jealous of him and wanted the throne to pass to her own son instead. The wicked woman schemed against Prince Rama. Eventually, she tricked the king into banishing his son from the palace for fourteen years!

So Prince Rama had to go and live in the forest – and of course his loyal princess willingly went with him. Sita had to swap her palace rooms decorated with gold and silver and jewels for a simple wooden hut, but she didn't mind, as long as her beloved prince was by her side. In fact, Sita loved the simplicity of life in the forest and felt more at peace with all the plants, creatures and birds there than she had surrounded by courtiers in the palace.

But unfortunately for Sita and her prince, the forest wasn't an ordinary forest. It was home to many demons – not least, the terrible ten-headed demon king, Ravana! From the moment Ravana laid his greedy eyes on the beautiful Sita, he wanted her for himself. From that moment on, he plotted how he might kidnap her.

One day, Sita and Rama were sitting outside their little hut in the company of Rama's younger brother, Prince Lakshmana. Suddenly, Sita noticed a flash of gold among the green of the trees. She immediately stopped chatting and silently touched Prince Rama's hand, to quiet him too. He and his brother immediately fell silent, hardly daring to breathe. For there, grazing in the undergrowth, was a gleaming golden deer! The unique animal was so beautiful that Sita could not take her eyes off it! "Oh please, Rama," she whispered, "please capture the creature for me! I have never seen anything so wonderful. I could look after it here and protect it from all the dangers of the forest."

Rama looked into his princess's big, beseeching eyes, and found himself agreeing to her request. "Very well," he whispered back, "but I am most uneasy about it. Something is not right about that deer – there may be black magic at work. My princess, I will do as you ask – but only if you promise me that you will stay right by Lakshmana's side and do exactly as he says. I trust him to protect you."

The princess nodded her agreement excitedly, her eyes shining. Rama turned and began to move stealthily through the trees towards the point where the deer stood. Even though the prince was utterly silent, the deer suddenly looked up sharply and noticed him. In a split second it had taken fright and was off into the bushes. Prince Rama took off at top speed, in hot pursuit.

The princess and Prince Lakshmana watched him disappear into the shady green depths of the forest. "I wonder how long it will take him to track the deer down," Sita wondered aloud.

But it wasn't long before the pair heard a bloodchilling yell and Prince Rama's voice calling out, "Help! Help me!"

Sita and Lakshmana looked at each other in alarm. "He's in trouble!" the princess gasped. "I must go to him at once!" She stood up, about to dart away, but Lakshmana stopped her.

"No, princess!" he commanded in a firm voice. "I don't believe that that really is my brother. It must be some sort of trick. You should stay here and I will go to investigate. But first..." Lakshmana quickly reached for a piece of chalk from the path nearby and swiftly drew a circle around the princess and the hut, with him on the outside. He closed his eyes and muttered a strange spell. "There," the young prince said, "now you will be safe. No one can cross the line and enter the circle

– and you must not cross the line and leave it, under any circumstances."

Sita gave Lakshmana an anxious smile in agreement. The prince then grabbed his bow and arrows and sped off in the direction of the voice.

The princess was left all alone in the forest, standing inside the magic circle. How helpless she felt, waiting there, wondering if her prince was suffering – or even dead! As she stood, wringing her hands with fear, an aged holy man came shuffling through the trees. He held out a bowl towards her. "Please give me a little food, I beg of you, and I promise to pray for you in return," he said.

Of course, the generous, kind-hearted Sita didn't think twice. She hurried into the hut and came out with some food. But how was she to give it to the old man? He could not

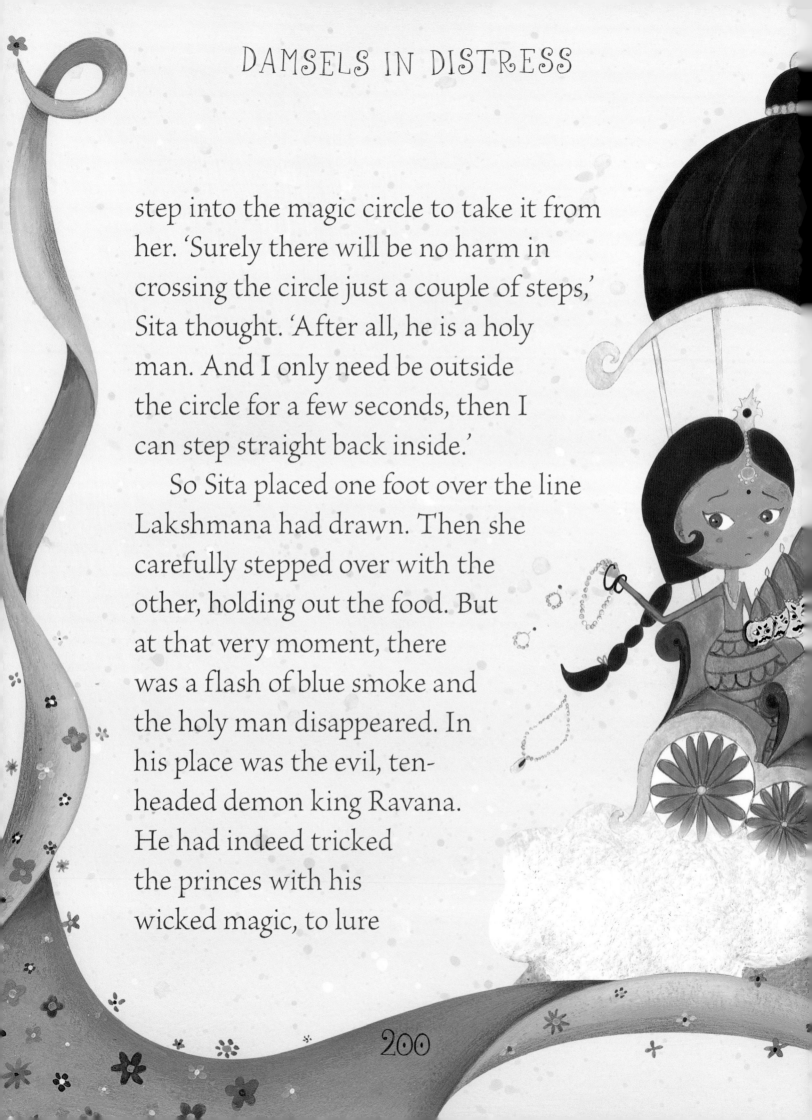

step into the magic circle to take it from her. 'Surely there will be no harm in crossing the circle just a couple of steps,' Sita thought. 'After all, he is a holy man. And I only need be outside the circle for a few seconds, then I can step straight back inside.'

So Sita placed one foot over the line Lakshmana had drawn. Then she carefully stepped over with the other, holding out the food. But at that very moment, there was a flash of blue smoke and the holy man disappeared. In his place was the evil, ten-headed demon king Ravana. He had indeed tricked the princes with his wicked magic, to lure

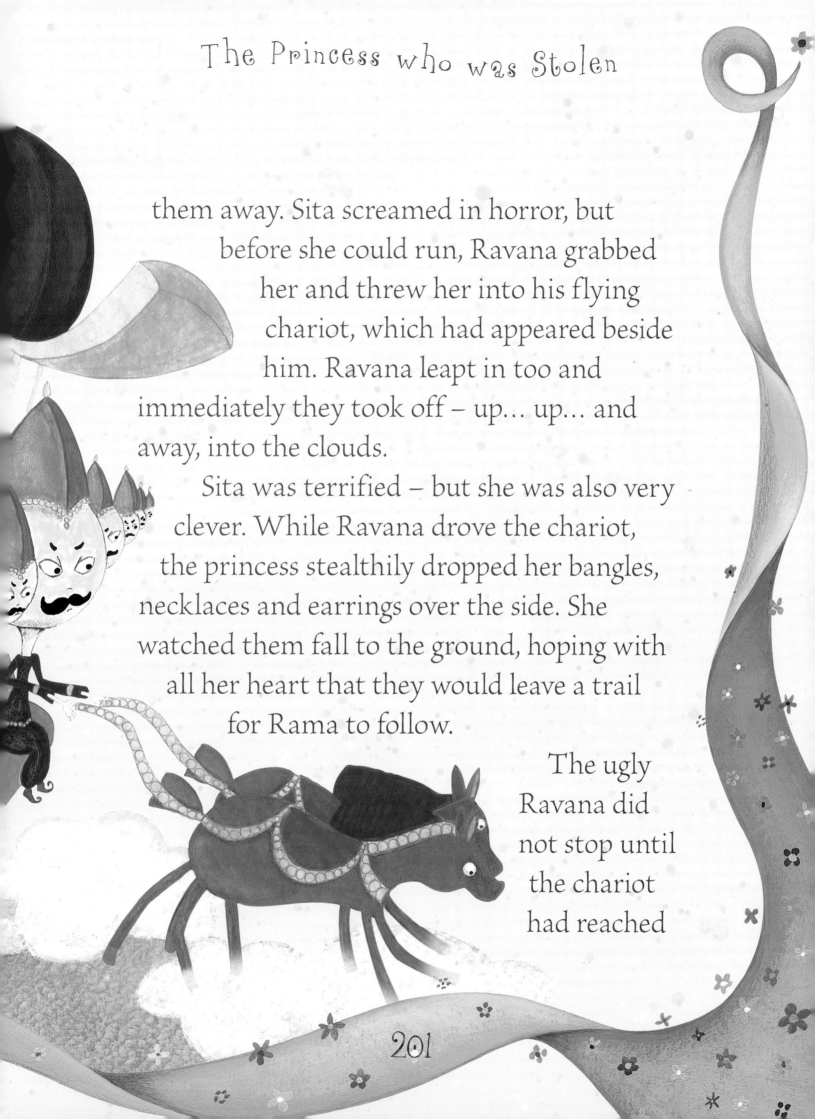

them away. Sita screamed in horror, but
before she could run, Ravana grabbed
her and threw her into his flying
chariot, which had appeared beside
him. Ravana leapt in too and
immediately they took off – up… up… and
away, into the clouds.

Sita was terrified – but she was also very
clever. While Ravana drove the chariot,
the princess stealthily dropped her bangles,
necklaces and earrings over the side. She
watched them fall to the ground, hoping with
all her heart that they would leave a trail
for Rama to follow.

The ugly
Ravana did
not stop until
the chariot
had reached

his demon kingdom, Lanka. There, he took Sita to a garden of Ashoka trees and commanded a group of hideous demonesses to watch over her. "If she escapes, I will torture every one of you for centuries!" the demon king hissed.

And so Sita was held captive. Days went by, then months, then a year. And all that time she waited, praying that Rama would find her. But there was no sign of him.

One evening, while the princess sat gazing sadly up at the stars, a shadowy figure came creeping silently up to her. It was the king of the magic monkey warriors, Hanuman! He gave her the message she had been hoping for for so long – Rama was looking for her. "Take heart, princess!" he told her. "It will not be long now until you are rescued!"

And soon, Hanuman's words were proved

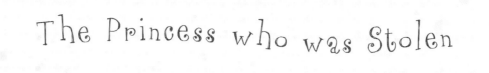

true. He and his monkey warriors had helped Prince Rama to build a bridge across the dark, wild sea that surrounded the demon king's realm. When it was finished, Prince Rama crossed the bridge and attacked, with brave Prince Lakshmana as his second-in-command, and an army of magic monkey warriors and faithful bear soldiers. A bloody

battle raged for a long time, and many thousands of these brave creatures perished. But at last, Rama shot a magic arrow through the heart of the wicked demon king. The ugly Ravana sank to the ground, dead. Then the monkeys and bears raced off and searched throughout Lanka until they found Sita. The princess was set free at last!

Now, I could tell you of Sita and Rama's tearful reunion. I could tell you how the princess proved her love for her prince by walking through a fire, and that the flames refused to burn her and turned to flower petals as she passed. And I could tell you how, as the brave band left Lanka, the bridge sank into the sea so no one could return to the demon kingdom. But all this is another story.

Suffice to say that everyone rejoiced as the princess, the princes and the animal warriors passed by on their journey home. The people of India lit little lamps of many colours and placed them on their doorsteps and in their windows to light their way. And we still remember the triumphant return of Princess Sita today, in the festival of lights we know as Divali.

The Princess who Would Not Smile

Retold from Alexander Afanasev's
version of a Russian folk tale

If you think about it, what a big world this is. In it live all sorts of folk – young and old, clever and foolish, rich and poor. Every person has their lot, but God watches over and judges them all.

In the Tsar's palace, the Princess Without a Smile grew fairer every day. What a life she had, what riches and what beauty all around her! She had everything she could wish for –

and more besides. But the princess never smiled, and never laughed. It seemed as though her heart was not capable of rejoicing at anything.

It was a very bitter thing for the Tsar, her father, to gaze at his doleful daughter. So one day he threw open the gates of the imperial palace to whoever wished to be his guest. "Come," he announced to all the men in his kingdom – and all the neighbouring kingdoms round about, "come and try to cheer up the Princess Without a Smile. Anyone who succeeds shall have her hand in marriage."

As soon as the proclamation had been made, all sorts of men began arriving at the palace. They came riding and walking from all directions – princes and princes' sons, noblemen and merchants, soldiers and farmers… and what great feasts were held for

them at the palace!
The king introduced
each and every one
of them to the
princess, and they
all did their utmost
to make her smile.
Many of them told
jokes, some pulled
funny faces. Others
tried to surprise her
with magic tricks
and acrobatics. One
young man even sat and stared at
the princess... and stared... and
stared... and stared... hoping that her
stony face would break before his did. But
still, she would not smile for any of them.

Now in a distant land, in a shabby little

hut, there lived a poor workman. Every morning before the sun came up he hurried to his master's farm. There, he would sweep the courtyard before everyone was awake and then set about all the jobs that needed doing – tending the corn, grooming the horses, repairing the barns, and so on. Every evening, before he could go home, he had to take the cattle out to pasture. And so he slaved away from dawn till dusk.

His master was a rich man, but a fair man. After the workman had been working for him for a year, he put a purse stuffed with money on the table. "You have worked very hard for me," he said to the labourer. "Take as much as you like." And then he went outside, leaving the workman to it.

The workman went up to the table and weighed the heavy purse in his hand. He was a good, God-fearing man, and he thought to himself, 'It would be wrong to be greedy and take too much'. So he took just one coin, which he held tight in his palm. But as he left his master's house, he stopped at the well in the courtyard for a drink – and the coin slipped through his fingers and fell to the bottom. The workman was left with nothing.

Now, anybody else in his position would have been very fed up and angry, but the workman was not at all. "God is in charge of everything," he said to himself. "The Lord knows what he gives to each person and why – and what he takes away too. Obviously, this is a sign from God that I have not been doing a very good job. I mustn't get angry – I must accept it and try again. But this time, I need to do better."

So the workman went back to work for the

rich man. And this time, he worked even faster and tried even harder at all his tasks than before. When another year was up, his master put a big, heavy bag of money on the table. "Do take as much as you want," he said and went out, leaving the workman to it.

Again, the workman thought it would be wrong to be greedy and take too much. So he took one coin from the bag. As he was leaving, he went to have a little drink at the well. But – would you believe it! – in some way or another, this coin also tumbled from his hand and was lost in the well.

So the workman went back to work for the rich man once more, even more determinedly than before. He worked so hard that often he toiled right through the night, not sleeping. And during the day, he was so busy at his tasks that he often forgot to eat. His master's corn grew tall and golden, while the corn of other landowners nearby was dry and pale. His master's cattle frisked down the lane, while the cattle of other landowners plodded lazily. His master's horses pranced and tossed their manes, while the horses of other landowners stumbled along. His master's barns stood strongly, freshly painted, while the barns of other landowners looked shabby and tumbledown.

The rich man knew very well whom he should thank for the success of his farm. When the third year came to an end, he put a great sack of money on the table. "Please take as much as you want," he said and went outside, leaving the workman to it.

Once more, the workman took a single coin and then went to the well for a drink. But this time, as he drew up the water, the lost money floated up to the surface! He took the two coins, overjoyed. He felt sure that it was God's

reward for his labours. 'Now at last it's time for me to go out into the world and seek my fortune,' he thought to himself. So he set off happily down the road with the three coins in his pocket, going wherever his feet took him.

While passing through a field one day, a little mouse came running up to him and said: "Dear stranger, give me a coin and I promise I will be of service to you."

So the workman gave the mouse a coin.

Next he travelled through a forest, where a beetle crept up to him and said: "Dear stranger, give me a coin and I promise I will be of service to you."

So the workman gave the beetle his second coin.

Then he came to a pond, where a frog bounded up to him and said: "Dear stranger, give me a coin and I promise I will be of service to you."

So the workman gave the frog his last coin.

Finally he came to a great city. It was so

crowded! There were busy, bustling crowds of people and huge buildings all around. The workman turned in all directions, not knowing where to go. In front of him stood the Tsar's palace, gleaming gold and silver. With a start, the workman realized that at a window sat the Princess Without a Smile – and she was looking directly at him! Whatever should he do? He grew so embarrassed that his head span. Losing his balance, he fell and toppled straight over into the mud – *SPLAT!*

All at once, up bounded the frog, with the beetle and the mouse scurrying after him. They sprang to the workman's aid, cleaning him up as best they could. The little mouse dragged his coat off with her tiny teeth and tried to shake it out. The beetle crawled all over his boots, polishing them with her wings

until they were clean. And the frog shot out
his tongue, this way and that, eating up all the
flies that now buzzed around the workman.

The Princess Without a Smile looked on at the kind little creatures bustling about so intently – and she smiled.

At that very moment, the king entered her room with several newly-arrived princes. He could not believe his eyes. "Who has managed to cheer up my daughter?" he cried.

"It must have been me, when I entered the room," said one prince.

"No, it was when she saw me come in," argued another.

But, "No," said the princess, "it was the sight of that man there," and she pointed out the workman in the street.

The king was true to his word, so the workman was at once brought before the king, still flustered and covered in mud. To the workman's utter astonishment, he learned that he had made the princess smile, and so he was to marry her and be made a prince! He was delighted after his years of labour. So the couple were married with much celebration and lived smilingly ever after.

And I can assure you, this is a true story, every word of it.

The Goose-girl

Retold from the Grimm brothers'
version of a German fairytale

Once upon a time there lived a queen whose husband had been dead for many years. She had a beautiful daughter, whom she loved dearly.

When the princess grew up, her uncle arranged that she should marry a prince who lived in a distant country. It nearly broke the queen's heart to think that the princess would be living so far away. However, she knew that the prince was a good man and would make her daughter very happy. So the queen gave the princess all the gifts she could possibly wish for – jewellery and fine dresses and paintings and books. She also gave her the very finest treasure she possessed – a horse called Falada, which could talk.

The time came when the queen and the princess had to say a sorrowful goodbye. Then the princess and her waiting-maid mounted their horses and rode away down the road.

After they had travelled for a while, the princess began to feel very thirsty. She asked her waiting-maid to go to a nearby stream and fetch her a drink of water in her golden cup. "Get it yourself!" the girl replied, rudely. Shocked, the princess climbed down from her horse and went and sat by the stream, scooping up the water.

When she returned to her horse, she found her waiting-maid sitting in the saddle. "I want to ride Falada – you can ride my old nag," she said. The princess was taken aback – after all, no one had ever spoken to her like that before! She didn't know what to say or do, so she just made herself content with the waiting-maid's bony old pony.

Worse was to come. That evening, the maid forced the princess to swap her royal clothes for the maid's own shabby dress. The maid threatened to kill the princess if she told anyone – and she said it with such steely eyes and such an icy voice that the princess believed her.

So they journeyed on – with the maid wearing the princess's clothes and riding the princess's horse, and the princess following on behind dressed as the maid.

However, Falada the talking horse had seen everything, though he said nothing.

Eventually, the travellers reached the far-off country that was home to the prince, and made their way to the palace. All the court rejoiced when they arrived and the prince dashed out to welcome his bride. He helped the waiting-maid down from Falada and escorted her into the palace, thinking she was the princess.

Meanwhile, the old king looked out of the window and saw the real princess standing in the courtyard. He thought she was beautiful and graceful, and asked the prince's bride who she was. "Oh she's just a maid," the wicked waiting-maid replied. "Give her some work to do – she may as well make herself useful."

The king didn't like the thought of such a lovely girl doing any hard or horrible tasks, so he sent her to help a young boy called Conrad look after the geese.

And so the princess set about her work, while preparations were underway for the wedding. Meanwhile, the false bride was busy getting to know the prince and doing her best to make him fall in love with her.

"I beg you to grant me a favour," she said to him one day.

"What is it, my darling?" the prince replied.

"I hate that horse I rode here on," the waiting-maid grumbled. "I want you to have it killed." Of course, she was worried that Falada would speak and tell everyone the truth.

The prince was rather alarmed. After all, it seemed like a terribly violent thing to ask for – and as far as he could tell, the horse had done nothing wrong! However, he didn't want to upset his bride just before they were married, so reluctantly he agreed.

When the real princess found out what was going to happen, she was frantic. She hurried to the slaughterman and paid him several pieces of gold to spare Falada. Then in the middle of the night when everyone was asleep, she crept away with the horse. She led him along the silent streets and out through the town gate. They came to a field nearby, which was quite hidden from the road by bushes, trees and high hedges. Here, the princess let Falada loose, and then she returned to the palace.

Early next morning, as usual, the princess and Conrad drove the flock of geese out through the gateway, on their way to the water meadows. As the princess passed the field, she couldn't help but let out a sigh. "Alas, Falada, hidden there!" she said sadly.

The horse replied, "Alas, young queen, how badly you fare! If this your tender mother knew, her heart would surely break in two."

The princess and Conrad carried on driving their geese out into the countryside. When they came to the water meadows, the princess sat down to rest and untied her long hair. It hung down to her waist like spun silk and shone like pure gold. Conrad thought it was so beautiful that he decided to pull a strand out

for himself. But the princess saw what he was about to do and called out, "Blow, blow, thou gentle wind. I say, blow Conrad's little hat away, and make him chase it here and there, until once more I have braided my hair."

At this there came such a strong gust of wind that it blew Conrad's hat far away, and he was forced to run after it. By the time he had caught it and returned, the princess had finished combing her hair and was putting it up again, so he could not get any of it. This made Conrad so angry that he would not speak to her. And so they watched the geese in silence until the evening and then went back to the palace.

The next day, everything happened just the same… and on the next day. But on the evening of the third day, Conrad stomped off to see the king when they returned. "I won't tend the geese with that girl any longer!" he told him.

"Why not?" asked the old king.

"Because she's so annoying!" said Conrad, and he told the king all about how the princess spoke with the horse by the town gate and made his hat blow away over the water meadow.

The old king scratched his beard and was silent for a few minutes, thinking. Then he looked up at Conrad with a twinkle in his eye.

He commanded the boy to drive his flock out the next morning as usual. And when dawn came, the king went and hid by the town gate and watched for himself. He saw the strange happenings with his own eyes, and when the goose-girl came home that evening, he called her to him and asked her to explain why she did these things.

Of course, she couldn't tell the king what was going on. "If I do, I will be killed," the goose-girl said sadly, shaking her head.

The old king tried his best to get the truth from her, to no avail. "If you can't speak to me, why don't you talk to that iron stove over there," he said eventually, and left the room.

The princess crept over to the iron stove and knelt next to it. She spoke to it as if it were a close friend, weeping and telling the whole story. Little did she know that the old

king was
standing outside
by the stove pipe listening to every word!

The king hurried back in and ordered his servants to dress the girl in royal clothes at once – and how beautiful she was! Then he called his son and told him that the girl he thought was his bride was actually the waiting-maid – and a wicked one at that!

When the prince saw the beautiful, graceful goose-girl he fell deeply in love with her. The wicked waiting-maid was banished from the kingdom forever, forced to leave on her bony old pony.

A magnificent wedding was soon held for the prince and the goose-girl, and they reigned over their land with peace and happiness for many years.

BRAVE, WISE AND TRUE

The Wild Swans

Retold from a story by Hans Christian Andersen

Long ago, there lived a king who had eleven sons and a little daughter, Eliza. Sadly, their mother died and after a while, the king married again. His new bride was evil and hated the children. She bewitched the king so he no longer noticed them, and then sent Eliza away to live with a woodcutter in a shack in the forest. Finally, she pointed her bony finger at the princes and cried: "Fly out into the world and be gone!" At this, the princes were transformed into magnificent wild swans. They flew out of the palace windows and off over the forest, away to the sea.

Many years passed and poor Eliza longed for her family every day. The woodcutter told her what had happened to her brothers and, when she was eighteen, she made up her mind to go and search for them.

Eliza wandered through the forest for many days, until at last she came to the wide sea. She felt as though she had reached the world's end. When the sun was setting, Eliza suddenly caught sight of eleven great swans with crowns on their heads, flying across the water towards her. She quickly hid behind some rocks. The swans landed as the sun disappeared beneath the waves. Then their feathers disappeared and there stood eleven handsome princes – Eliza's brothers! She raced to them and they all wept with joy.

"The queen enchanted us," the princes explained to Eliza. "While it is daylight, we must fly about as wild swans. But as soon as the sun sets, we become human once more. The queen has banished us to live in a country which lies across this ocean – we can only come back here to our homeland once each year, to catch a glimpse of our father in the castle. Tomorrow, we must journey back

across the sea. Will you come with us?"

"Oh yes, please," sighed Eliza.

The princes spent the night weaving a net of willow bark and reeds. Then at sunrise, Eliza lay in it and the swans lifted it in their beaks and flew with her across the sea. On they went, until they reached land and swooped down. After sunset, the princes showed Eliza their home – a cave filled with thick moss, like a green carpet.

That night, Eliza had the strangest dream – a fairy came to her and told her how to free her brothers. "You must weave stinging nettles into eleven shirts, to cover your brothers," the fairy explained. "But you must use your bare hands, even though the nettles will sting them. And you must not speak a word until you are finished…"

The moment Eliza woke, she rushed out of the cave to begin her work. Her brothers were very shocked, especially because she could not talk – but they knew she must be up to something. After two weeks, one shirt was finished. Eliza then began the second…

That day, while the swans were off flying, a pack of hunting dogs burst through the trees, closely followed by nobles on galloping horses. Eliza fled in terror into the cave, but the most handsome man came and found her.

He was a prince – and he had never seen a more beautiful girl. "Who are you and where did you come from?" he asked Eliza gently. But of course, she could not say a word. She just shook her head. The prince took Eliza and lifted her onto his horse. He galloped her back to the castle, to look after her.

When the ladies-in-waiting had bathed Eliza and dressed her in royal robes, she looked dazzlingly beautiful. But her face was sadder than ever. Then the prince led her to her bedroom. It was decorated green, just like the cave, and in it were her nettles and the shirt she had already woven. Eliza flung her arms around the prince's neck and kissed him, smiling joyfully.

Days went by and Eliza fell just as deeply in love with the kind prince as he was with her, although she still did not dare speak a word. He did everything to make her happy, and it was soon announced that they were getting married!

All the people rejoiced – except for the prince's chief priest, the archbishop. "This wild girl from the forest who cannot speak must be a witch!" he whispered into the prince's ear.

"She has put you under her spell." But the prince refused to listen.

How Eliza longed to tell the prince what she was doing. But of course, she could not, so instead she got on with her work in silence. Eventually, ten shirts were finished – but she did not have enough nettles for the eleventh. She knew that more grew out in the churchyard – but how would she ask for them? It was no good, she would have to go and fetch them herself.

That night, Eliza slipped out to the churchyard. There, a terrifying sight met her eyes – a coven of witches sat hunched over the tombstones, stirring up evil spells in the moonlight. Eliza said a silent prayer and hurried past them, then gathered up some nettles and dashed back to the castle.

Little did she know, the archbishop had

followed her and seen everything. "I knew it!" he murmured. "She's a witch!" He went straight to the prince and told him what he had seen. "She has bewitched you – see for yourself," he insisted. "Just wait till this evening – maybe she will go to meet her witch friends again."

Eliza did indeed need more nettles and that night slipped out once more to the churchyard. The archbishop and the prince followed her at a distance – and unfortunately it did look as though she was meeting up with the witches.

The prince was heartbroken. The punishment for being a witch was to be burnt at the stake! But there was nothing he could do. He had to follow his own laws, even though he loved Eliza with all his heart.

Soldiers were immediately sent to arrest

Eliza. She was taken to a dark, dreary cell, where the wind whistled though the iron bars. She was at least allowed to bring the nettle shirts with her, and so she spent the rest of the night working away determinedly at the eleventh.

The next morning, the soldiers came again for Eliza, and along with the nettle shirts, they led her to a big bonfire. All the people stood sadly around, for they could not believe that the lovely Eliza was a witch. But the archbishop seemed excited and pleased as he strode over to light the flames.

All of a sudden, there was a great rush of air. Eleven mighty wild swans came flying around Eliza, beating the archbishop back with their huge wings. Silently, Eliza threw a nettle shirt over each one. To everyone's amazement, the swans began to transform until eleven handsome princes stood there. However, the youngest still had a swan's wing instead of one arm, for Eliza had not quite managed to finish the last sleeve.

"Now I may speak!" Eliza cried. "I am innocent!" She and her brothers explained everything to the prince and the crowd.

The prince ordered that the wicked archbishop should be hauled away to his deepest, darkest dungeon. He and Eliza were married in the most magnificent wedding anyone had ever seen, and they brought her brothers to live with them in the castle, happily ever after.

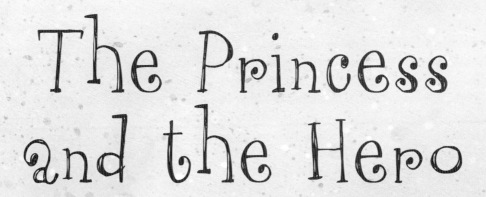

The Princess and the Hero

Retold from Nathaniel Hawthorne's
version of a Greek myth

*L*ong ago, in the lands of ancient Greece, there lived a young man called Theseus, the son of King Aegeus of Athens. He was exceedingly brave, strong and daring, and his ambition was to perform many heroic deeds, so his fame would live forever.

As soon as Theseus was old enough, he volunteered for a truly terrible task. Once every year, his father was forced to send a gift to a neighbouring king, Minos, to keep him from invading Athens. The gift was seven young men and seven young women – they were sent to feed a dreadful monster who was half-man, half-bull, called the Minotaur. It lived in a terrifying underground maze called the labyrinth.

"This year, I myself will be the seventh young man," declared Prince Theseus. "I swear that I will kill this evil Minotaur – or die in the attempt!"

Old King Aegeus shed many tears and begged his beloved son not to go. But Theseus insisted. "You cannot expect your subjects to give up their sons and daughters if you are not prepared to give up your own," he argued.

So the old king was forced to let him go.

Just like the years before, a ship was rigged with black sails. A crowd of weeping people

accompanied Theseus, along with six other young men and seven young women, down to the harbour. They set sail.

When the ship arrived in King Minos's kingdom, guards were waiting in the harbour to escort the despairing men and women to the palace. There, King Minos himself was waiting for them. Now, King Minos was an evil, ruthless king. He had a heart so cold and cruel it was as if it were made of iron. He keenly poked and prodded each young person to make sure they were plump enough for the Minotaur.

Next to the king's throne stood his daughter, Ariadne. The princess was as kind-hearted as her father was cruel. She sobbed quietly as she looked upon the trembling young people who were soon to be devoured by the hideous monster. Then her eyes fell upon the brave, calm figure of Prince Theseus, and she felt a hundred times more pity than before. As the guards started to take the captives away, she flung herself at the king's feet and begged him to set them all free.

"Peace, foolish girl!" bellowed King Minos. "This is none of your business!" He looked monstrous enough to rip Theseus and the other captives apart himself, right there and then.

So the prisoners were chained up in a cold, gloomy dungeon. The jailer advised them to go to sleep as soon as possible, because the Minotaur called for his breakfast early! The seven maidens and six of the young men sobbed themselves into a nightmare-filled sleep. But Theseus was different. He sat awake and alert, wracking his brains to come up with a plan that would save them all.

Just before midnight, Theseus heard a noise outside. The door was quietly unbarred, and to Theseus's astonishment, the gentle Princess Ariadne stood in the doorway with a flaming torch in her hand.

"Are you awake, Prince Theseus?" she whispered.

"Yes," he answered. "With so little time left to live, I'm not about to waste it sleeping."

The princess crossed the dungeon and

unlocked his chains. "Then follow me," she told him, "but tread softly."

What had become of the jailer and the guards, Theseus never knew – although he was sure it was Ariadne who had somehow got rid of them. She unlocked all the doors and led him out of the dark, stinking prison into the moonlight.

"Now you can get onboard your ship and sail home," the princess urged Theseus.

"No," answered the young man solemnly. "I will not leave unless I can first slay the Minotaur and save my poor companions."

"I knew you would say that," the princess said sadly. "Come with me."

From out of her cloak she drew a sword, which she handed to Theseus. Then she led him through a shadowy grove to a high marble wall. The wall seemed to have no door, but rose straight up, lofty and mysterious. Theseus couldn't see how anyone could either climb over it or pass through it. He watched, transfixed, as Ariadne pressed her finger against one of the blocks of marble and it slid open, making a narrow entrance. They crept through and the marble slid back into place.

Before them stood another wall, overgrown with creepers. There was an open doorway in the wall, through which only darkness could be seen.

"We are at the entrance to the labyrinth," whispered the princess. "If we were to take just a few steps inside, we might wander about for the rest of our lives and never find our way out. Yet in the very centre is the Minotaur."

"But however shall I find my way to him?" asked Theseus.

As he spoke, they heard a distant roar.

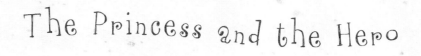

"That's him," whispered the princess, grasping Theseus's hand. "If you follow that sound through the windings of the labyrinth, you will find him. Take the end of this silk string. I will hold the other end. Then, if you

defeat him, you will be able to find your way out by following the string back here."

Thanks to the princess's courage and wisdom, the young prince felt hope surge in his heart. He took the end of the silk string in one hand, and with his sword in the other, stepped boldly into the labyrinth.

The maze was so dark that Theseus had not taken five steps before he lost sight of Ariadne. In five more, his head grew dizzy from the twisting and turning of the corridors. But still he went on, creeping through a low arch, climbing a flight of steps, now in one crooked passage and now in another, with here a door opening before him, and there one banging shut behind, until it really seemed as if the walls were spinning and whirling him round along with them.

All the while through these hollow

avenues, the roar of the Minotaur echoed.

Theseus would have felt quite lost and close to despair if, every now and again, he had not felt a gentle twitch at the silk string. Then he knew that Ariadne was still holding the other end, and that she was fearing for him, and hoping for him, and urging him on as though she were by his side.

At last, Theseus reached the very centre of the labyrinth. He came out into an open space and was met with the hideous sight of the Minotaur. He had the horned head of a bull and yet the body and legs of a man. He lumbered to and fro, letting out a fierce roar mixed with half-formed words. Theseus hated him – and yet pitied him too. As he listened, Theseus began to understand what the Minotaur was saying – that he was miserable and hungry; that he hated everybody and

wanted to eat up the entire human race.

Theseus suddenly felt a twitch of the silk string in his hand. It was as if Ariadne were giving him all her might and courage. And how he needed it, for the Minotaur lowered his horribly sharp horns and charged…

The fight that followed was the most ferocious duel ever seen beneath the sun or moon. The two were locked in a bloody battle, sword to horn, for a long while. At last, the Minotaur made a run at Theseus, gored his left side, and flung him to the floor. Thinking he had stabbed him to the heart, the Minotaur threw back his head, opened his mouth and prepared to rip the prince's head off. But Theseus leapt up and stabbed the beast in his exposed neck, so he crashed to the ground, dead.

Theseus leant on his sword, gasping for breath. And as he did so, he felt another twitch of the silk string – which he still held fast in his hand. Eagerly, he followed the thread back through the dizzying gloom – and to his huge relief found himself at the entrance to the labyrinth.

"I have slain the monster!" he cried, sweeping the overjoyed Ariadne into his arms. "But I could never have done it without you!"

"Quickly now," urged Ariadne, "we must rescue your friends. You must all be back on the ship before day breaks and my father discovers what you have done."

When the prince and princess woke the captives, they couldn't believe they weren't still dreaming. They hurried down to the harbour and back onto the black-sailed ship. Theseus stood on the quay, clasping Ariadne's hand in his own.

"My darling princess," he said, "you cannot stay here, for your father will punish you severely when he discovers how you have helped me. Besides… you must come with me or my heart will break."

So the noble and courageous Princess

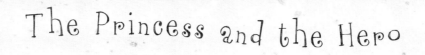

Ariadne gladly boarded the ship with the bold hero, Prince Theseus. And they sailed away from the wicked King Minos and his cruel kingdom forever.

The Little Mermaid

Retold from a story by Hans Christian Andersen

Far out in the ocean, where the water is as blue as cornflowers, it is very, very deep. There live the most lovely sea creatures and plants. In the deepest spot of all was a castle where the sea king lived with his six daughters. The sea princesses were all beautiful mermaids, but the youngest was loveliest of all.

Every day, the sea princesses played happily

in the castle or outside. Each mermaid had a
little garden to tend as she pleased. The
youngest mermaid grew flowers around the
statue of a handsome boy which had fallen
from a shipwreck. She loved to hear about the
world above – for the sea princesses were not
allowed to the surface to see it for themselves
until they were eighteen. The little mermaid
made her grandmother tell her everything she
knew about ships, towns and forests, as well as
the people and the animals.

Finally, the youngest princess's eighteenth
birthday came. How excited she was to rise to
the surface, light as a bubble! She raised her
head above the waves and gasped as she
caught sight of a grand ship floating in the
glorious sunset. The little mermaid swam
close and peered in through the cabin
windows. She saw people inside, eating and

drinking and dancing. Among them was a handsome young prince – it was his birthday party. As darkness came, coloured lanterns were lit on deck and the people came out to admire dazzling fireworks bursting in the sky.

The mermaid watched, fascinated, until it grew late. But then heavy clouds gathered overhead, thunder rumbled and lightning flashed, and the waves began to tower into dark mountains. The ship tossed and tipped, and suddenly plunged over on its side. Everyone was washed into the water!

To the little mermaid's horror, she saw the handsome prince sinking. His beautiful eyes were closed and she knew he was about to die. She dived and used all her strength to lift him and hold his head above the water.

When the sun rose, the little mermaid swam to a sandy bay and laid the prince in the

shallows. She stroked his wet hair and kissed his forehead – he seemed just like the statue in her garden. Then some girls came out of a nearby building, so the little mermaid quickly hid between some rocks. She watched as one of the girls spotted the prince and ran to him. The little mermaid saw him open his eyes and smile. Then the girl helped him up and led him away.

The little mermaid dived down and swam sorrowfully back to her father's castle. From that point on, her heart was filled with a great longing for the prince and the world above the waves. 'I will see if the sea witch can help me,' she thought.

The way to the sea witch's home was very dangerous. It lay through whirlpools, boiling mud and poisonous plants. When the brave little mermaid arrived, the witch said: "I know what you want. I will change your fish's tail into legs, so you can walk on land and find your prince. But every step will be as painful as treading on knives – and you will never be able to return to the sea and your family again. If the prince falls in love with you and marries you, you will become properly human, with a soul that will live in heaven after you die. But if he marries another girl, at sunrise on the next day your heart will break and you will become nothing but foam on the waves."

"I will do it," said the little mermaid, determinedly.

"But I must be paid," said the witch. "You have the sweetest voice in the ocean – give it to me."

"So be it," the little mermaid whispered.

The sea witch placed her cauldron on the fire, dropped in many evil ingredients, and prepared a magic potion in a bottle. She held up another bottle and conjured the mermaid's voice out into it, so she could enjoy it forever. Then the little mermaid silently took the magic potion and rose up, up, up, through the dark blue waters.

The moon shone brightly over the sandy bay, as the little mermaid floated in the shallows and drank the potion. It hurt as if she were swallowing fire, and she fainted.

When the sun rose, she came to. She was lying in the shallows and before her stood the handsome young prince, smiling. She looked down shyly – and realized that her tail was gone. Instead, she had a pretty pair of legs and feet and she was wearing clothes. The prince asked who she was and where she came from, but the mermaid just looked at him sorrowfully, for she could not speak. He

helped her to stand and walk, and every step she took was painful, but she didn't mind.

The prince took her back to the palace and looked after her, for she was the most beautiful girl he had ever seen. He was completely charmed by her and told her that she would stay with him always. Time passed, and every day the little mermaid was overjoyed to be with the prince – she only wished she could tell him.

But one morning, the little mermaid woke to hear church bells. "Today is my wedding day," the prince explained. "My father has ordered that I get married, to a girl who saved my life when I lay half-drowned on the beach."

The little mermaid felt as though her heart were already broken.

The wedding was held on a magnificent ship out at sea. The little mermaid was a bridesmaid and wore a gold silk dress. But her ears didn't hear the music playing and her eyes didn't see the colourful flags. Her mind was filled with everything she had given up, and of dying and becoming foam on the waves.

Late that night, the prince and his bride went to their cabin. The little mermaid turned to where the sun would rise and waited for the morning, when she was going to die.

As the first ray of dawn lit the sky, the little mermaid threw herself into the sea – but her body did not dissolve into foam. The sun rose and all around her floated beautiful transparent beings. The little mermaid suddenly realized that her body was like theirs, and she soared up into the sky.

"We are spirits," one of the beings explained. "We fly around the world doing good deeds. When we have done enough, we are granted a soul and go to live in heaven. You, little mermaid, have been chosen to join us, as you gave up everything you held dear for love."

The little mermaid's heart was filled with joy. She left the prince and his bride behind her, and flew away with the spirits to win her soul and be happy in heaven for ever.

The White Wolf

Retold from Andrew Lang's version
of an ancient fairytale

Once upon a time there was a king who had three daughters. They were all beautiful, but the youngest was the fairest.

One day, the king was on his way back from a distant part of his kingdom. He had bought presents for two of the princesses – a necklace for the eldest and a dress for the second – but he had nothing for his youngest daughter, for she had asked for a wreath of wild flowers and he had not found one.

When he was about four miles away from the palace, he noticed a big white wolf sitting by the roadside – and, look! – there on its head was a wreath of wild flowers.

The king ordered the carriage driver to stop at once. To his surprise, the wolf spoke to him. "O king," he said, "I will let you have the wreath, if you promise to give me the first living thing you meet on your way to the palace. In three days I shall come and fetch it."

'I am still a good way from home,' the king thought. 'I am sure to come across an animal or a bird on the road. It will be safe to make the promise.' So he agreed and carried the wreath away with him. However, to his horror, he didn't see a living creature at all along the road – until he turned into the palace gates and there was his youngest

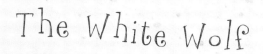

daughter waiting to welcome him.

The king was heartbroken – and the queen too, when he told her what had happened. Yet on the third day, when the wolf bounded into the palace, they had no choice but to hand over their youngest daughter. The wolf swung her onto his back, leapt out of the palace and was away into a deep forest.

He ran and ran and ran, until at last he stopped in front of a huge castle with enormous gates. The princess was very frightened, but as the gates swung open and she stepped inside, the white furry skin slipped from the wolf's body. She saw that he was not a wolf at all, but a handsome prince. He gave her his hand and led her up the castle steps. From then on he kept his human form, and treated the princess so kindly that she fell quite in love with him and lived at the castle most contentedly.

After half a year had passed, the prince one day said to her: "My dear one, your eldest sister is going to be married, so I will take you back to your father's palace. When the wedding is nearly over, I shall come to fetch you. When you hear me whistle outside the gate, come to me at once. For if I have to leave without you, you will never find your way back alone through the forest."

When the princess was ready to set off, she found that the prince had put on his white fur skin again. The wolf swung her onto his back, carried her to her father's palace and left her to enjoy the wedding. In the evening, during the feast, the princess heard a long, loud whistle. She left her family and went to the gate, and there was the wolf waiting. He swung her onto his back and carried her back to his castle.

The princess spent another half year very happily, until one day the prince told her: "Dear love, tomorrow I will take you to your father's palace for the wedding of your second sister. We will stay there together until the following morning."

So the wolf carried the princess to the

wedding and stayed with her at the feast. When the celebrations were over and the two were alone in their room together, his fur skin slipped off and he became a prince once more.

But little did either of them know that the princess's mother had hidden in their room. When the couple were asleep, the queen crept out of her hiding place, picked up the white skin and stole away. Then she burnt the skin in the kitchen fire.

The moment the flames touched the skin there was a fearful clap of thunder and the prince vanished in a sudden whirlwind. When the princess saw that he was gone, she was heartbroken and spent many hours weeping bitterly. She set out to find her own way back to his castle, but she wandered for fourteen days in the forest living on wild berries and roots, and could not find a track nor path to

guide her. In despair she asked the wind: "Wind, have you seen the white wolf?"

And the wind answered: "I have been blowing round the world, but I have not seen him." However, the wind gave her a pair of shoes in which she could walk a hundred miles with every step.

So the princess walked through the air until she reached a star. The star had not seen the white wolf, yet it gave her a pair of shoes in which she could

walk two hundred miles at a stride.

So next the princess walked to the moon. The moon had not seen the white wolf either, yet it gave her a pair of shoes in which she would be able to cover four hundred miles with every stride.

So the princess went to the sun and asked: "Sun, have you seen the white wolf?"

And the sun answered, "Yes, I have seen him. He is living in a palace at the top of a glass mountain – but he is under an enchantment that has made him forget all about you!" Then the sun gave the princess a pair of shoes in which she could walk on glass or ice and climb to the highest places. The sun also gave her a magic spinning wheel, which could spin moss into silk.

So the princess set off up the glass mountain. At its summit she found a palace, just as the sun had said. Great preparations were going on for a wedding the next day. Among all the hustle and bustle, the princess slipped inside without being noticed. There, to her dismay, she found that the wedding preparations were for her prince – who was about to marry a new bride!

The princess thought quickly and came up with a plan. She disguised herself as an old woman and sat spinning in the great hall, turning moss into silk. When the new bride passed by, she stopped to watch the spectacle, amazed. "What a wonderful spinning wheel!" she gasped. "Will you please sell it to me?"

And the princess answered, "I will give it to you for nothing if you will allow me to sleep tonight on the mat outside the prince's door."

The bride gladly agreed, so the princess gave her the spinning wheel. And that night, she lay down on the mat outside the prince's door. When everyone in the palace was fast asleep, the princess took off her disguise and began to whisper through the lock, telling the

whole of her story. How she was the youngest
of three sisters and that her father had
promised her to the white wolf; how they had
gone to a wedding and he had disappeared
when his fur skin was burnt; and how she had
searched for him for many days with the help
of the wind and the star and the moon and
the sun.

To her huge joy, the princess heard the door
unlocking. It opened and there stood her
prince, who clasped her in his arms as if he
would never let her go. The princess had
broken the enchantment by making the
prince remember everything. He promised
that they would never be parted again.

The next day, a wedding was held as
planned. But instead, it was the wedding of
the white wolf and the youngest princess. The
young lady he had been about to marry was

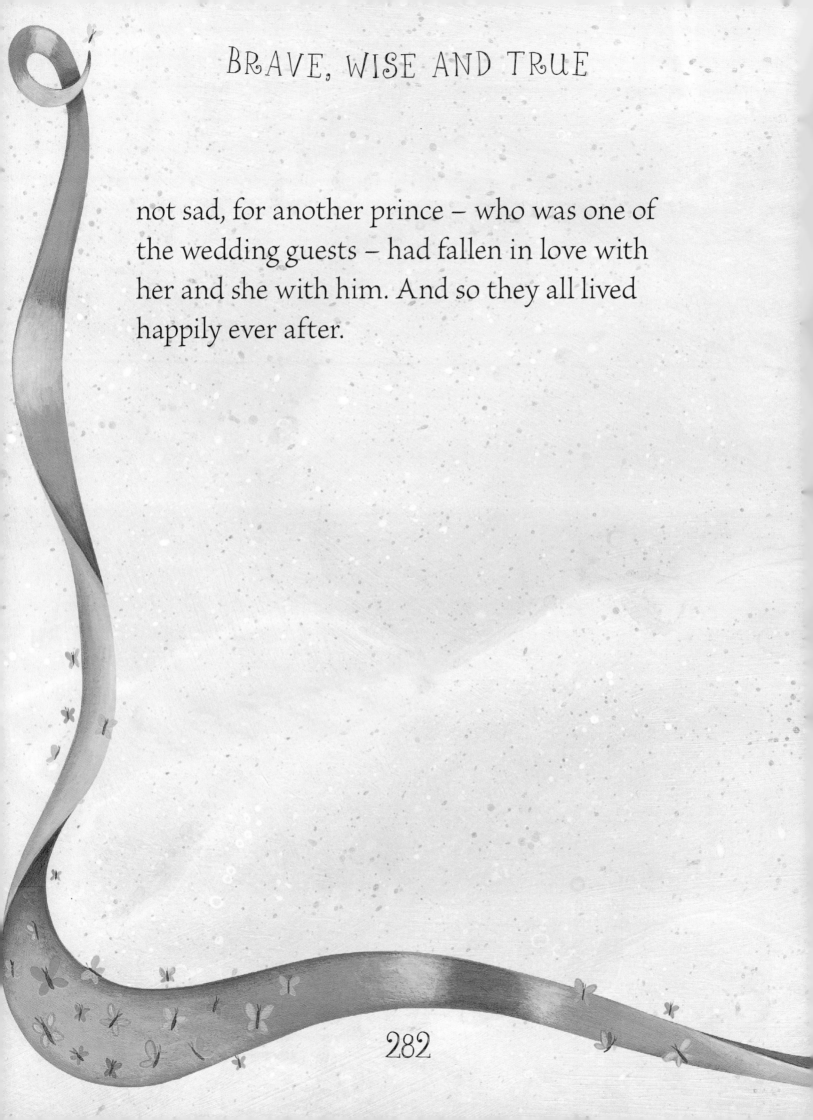

not sad, for another prince – who was one of the wedding guests – had fallen in love with her and she with him. And so they all lived happily ever after.

The Little Red Princess of the Forest

Retold from an account by
Frederick Winthrop Hutchinson

This is the story of a princess – not a fairy princess with a tiara and a silken gown, but a real princess. You wouldn't have known it if you had seen her running barefooted through the forest, because she was a little Native American girl, who played with other children in the woods of Virginia, North America. Yet this little girl was a princess and her father was a king.

283

The name of this princess was Pocahontas. It is a large name for a little girl; and, though it is three hundred years since she lived, no one has forgotten it. I will tell you why…

In those days, Virginia was very different from today. There were no cities, cars, schools nor parks. It was all wild countryside, with great rivers, and forests where no roads led, and all the people were Native Americans.

By the time Pocahontas turned twelve, she was so very good and kind and beautiful that all her tribe loved her. The women embroidered her skirts with bright-coloured feathers and beads. The men brought her presents of beautiful birds and little grey squirrels, which they caught in the forest.

Her father – King Powhatan – loved her most of all. Whenever he returned from a journey, his first question was always, "Where

is Pocahontas?" And when she ran to him, he patted her on the head and gave her some shells, which the Native Americans used for money. There was nothing in the world that the king would not do for her.

Pocahontas had never seen a white man. You see, there had never been any people from Europe in that part of the country. But one day the king's warriors brought into the village a strange prisoner. He was a tall man, with skin as white as milk, and light hair and blue eyes. The warriors shook their tomahawks in front of his face, but the man did not show any fear.

The Native Americans liked a brave man – and they thought this man seemed very brave indeed. Pocahontas, who was watching from the door of her father's teepee, thought him brave too. She saw how the thongs of deer-skin, with which he was bound, cut into his white skin, so she asked her father to order the prisoner to be untied, and this he did.

The man was a courageous English soldier called Captain John Smith. He had been a solider since he was very young, and had fought bravely in several wars before being sent to North America. He and his little band of men had sailed up the James River in Virginia and started to build a settlement called Jamestown. However, Captain Smith did not have enough for his men to eat – and they did not want to work for it. They wanted to find gold and silver and become rich right away – they did not want to plant corn and build houses, barns and forts. They ran into trouble with the Native Americans who lived there, and Smith had been captured.

King Powhatan and his tribe were curious to know all about the white men. They spent long hours examining Captain Smith, learning to communicate with him. He showed them writing and reading, and the Native Americans marvelled at it. Smith showed them his compass and demonstrated that with it, he would never be lost. Many of the Native Americans thought that the compass was magic and grew fearful of him, but Pocahontas was not afraid. She loved hearing

Smith's stories of a country called England, across the sea, and she grew very fond of him. Eventually, King Powhatan called his warriors together to decide what to do with

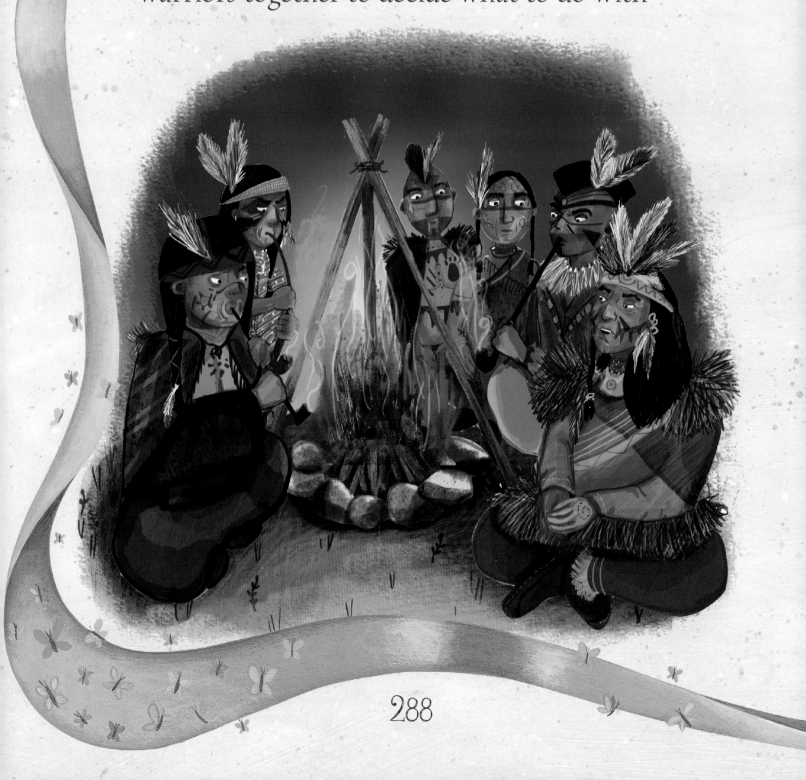

their captive. They all sat around a great campfire and each man smoked a long pipe. After a while, a very old and wise chief spoke up. "Oh, King Powhatan, it is not safe to let this man live," he said. "He is the friend of the devils – or how else could he talk with little marks or with the stars? The white man must be put to death."

There was a low murmur around the fire – many of the other warriors agreed. And so it was decided. King Powhatan had to abide by the wishes of his chiefs.

Pocahontas was very sad when she heard this. The man who had become her friend must die a cruel death, far from the country he loved.

All day she walked in the forest, desperately trying to think of some plan by which she could save his life. But when night approached, she had to return unhappily to camp without an answer. As Pocahontas neared the village, she met a young brave covered in his bright warpaint. "Hurry, oh princess," he said, "for the white man is to die at sundown."

At this, Pocahontas ran even more swiftly than the young brave. She reached her father's teepee just in time to see John Smith, bound hand and foot and stretched on the ground, waiting to be slain. All the Native Americans made way for the princess as she pushed through them. She fell on her knees and threw her arms around the captain's neck – anyone who wanted to kill him would have to kill her, too. She begged her father, the king, to give her Smith's life.

Powhatan and all the chiefs looked at the young girl kneeling before them, ready to die

to save her friend. They were greatly impressed at her bravery. "Let the white man go free," the king declared, and the Native Americans all grunted, which meant that they, too, were happy to reward Pocahontas in this way.

So John Smith rose from the ground a free man, and was sent with twelve braves back to Jamestown.

Yet this was not the only time that the little red princess saved the life of her friend. The Jamestown settlement was always in danger of attacks by other tribes. More than once, Pocahontas slipped through the great forest at night to warn Captain Smith that his enemies were coming. She also helped him by asking her father to send him corn. Without this, Smith and his men would certainly have starved.

But one day, when Pocahontas went to visit Jamestown, she found that Captain Smith had gone back to England to be cured of a wound. This made her very sad, although she still went often to Jamestown to hear news of her friend. In this way, she met a young Englishman named John Rolfe. After some years, Pocahontas and John Rolfe were married, and all the members of her tribe came to see the wedding.

So, in the fullness of time, Pocahontas came to cross the ocean to England. And in the great city of London, Pocahontas joyfully met her old friend, John Smith, once more! They had many happy times together.

It soon happened that everyone in London was talking about Pocahontas. The people there had never seen such a princess before, especially a princess who had done so many brave deeds and saved the lives of so many Englishmen. Everyone wished to honour her – even the king and queen sent for her! She was often at their court, where all the great lords and ladies loved her and gave her many beautiful presents.

At last, the time came for John Rolfe to go back to Jamestown. Pocahontas was very sad at the thought of leaving England and all her kind new friends. She was worried too, because she had had a little son, who must also make the long, rough journey. But their plans were laid and the ship was made ready to sail.

Yet it happened that at the very last moment, poor Pocahontas was taken ill. All the great doctors of London came to see her, but sadly their medicines were of no use. After a few days of suffering, she died. John

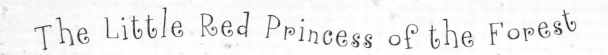

Rolfe buried her in England. But perhaps her spirit found its way back to the great silent woods of Virginia, where for so long she had lived with her tribe as the little red princess of the forest.

The Dirty Shepherdess

Rewritten from Andrew Lang's
version of a French folk tale

Once upon a time there lived a king who had two daughters. He loved them truly, with all his heart. One day, when the princesses were grown up, the king was suddenly seized with a burning desire to find out if his daughters felt the same. He decided to put them to the test.

First, the king called the elder princess to him and asked, "How much do you love me?"

"I love you as much as gold!" she answered.

"Ah!" exclaimed the king, kissing her tenderly, for that sounded like she loved him a lot. "You are indeed a good daughter."

Then the king sent for the younger princess, and asked her in turn, "How much do you love me?"

"My father," the girl answered, "I love you as much as salt."

"What sort of an answer is that?" bellowed the king angrily. "You could have said you love me as much as diamonds or the sun, but instead, you say you love me as much as salt! You are rude and ungrateful, and you obviously don't love me at all!" And he ordered the younger princess to leave the castle and never come back.

The poor princess was shocked and very upset, but she did as she was told. She hurried

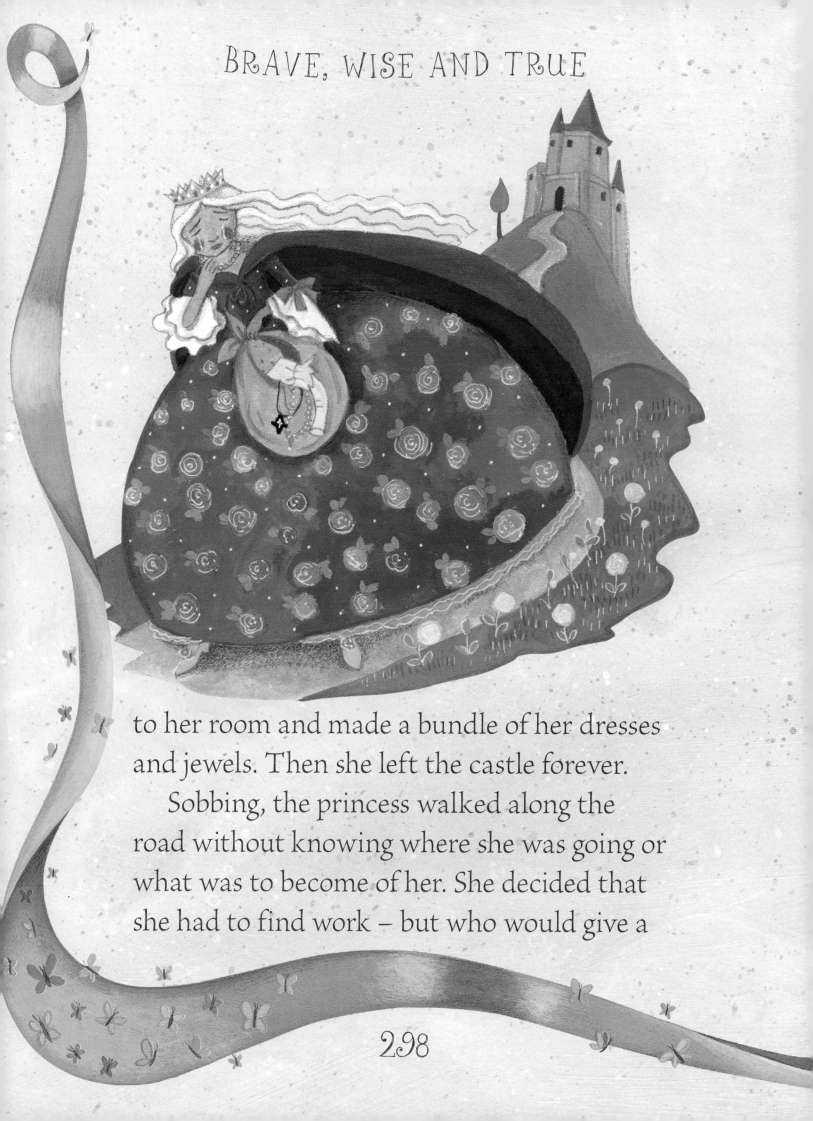

to her room and made a bundle of her dresses
and jewels. Then she left the castle forever.

Sobbing, the princess walked along the
road without knowing where she was going or
what was to become of her. She decided that
she had to find work – but who would give a

princess a job? The girl took off her silk robe and put on the plain cotton smock she wore while painting at her easel. She ripped the hem and sleeves and smudged it with dirt. Then she shook her hair into a great tangle and swapped her dainty embroidered slippers for bare feet.

Now disguised, the princess went about offering herself as a goose-girl or scullery maid. But no one took pity on her until, after walking for a great many days, she finally came to a large farm. The farmer had plenty of labourers but was in need of a shepherdess. So the princess gratefully set about looking after his flock, in return for food and a bed in the attic.

And with great sadness that was how the princess faced up to spending the rest of her days. She tried hard not to think about her father and sister and friends back at the castle, for every time she did so she felt as if her heart would break. But one day, while minding her flock high on a lonely mountainside, she drifted into remembering her joyful life as a princess.

She was all alone and did not think it would hurt if, just this once, she washed in a nearby stream and put on one of the beautiful robes from her bundle. In no time at all, she was once again transformed into a princess.

Little did she know that a prince from a neighbouring country had ventured into the mountains on a hunting trip. He was far off, but caught sight of the shepherdess in the distance. He thought she looked so beautiful that he had to meet her. He rode closer, but as soon as the girl noticed him coming, she fled into the woods. The prince chased after her,

but his horse caught a hoof on the root of a tree and stumbled, throwing him off. By the time he had picked himself up, the girl had vanished.

The disappointed prince, who was by this time both hot and thirsty, made his way to the farm nearby. There, he asked for a drink of water, but also inquired the name of the beautiful young lady that kept the sheep. At this all the farmworkers laughed, for the shepherdess was so tatty and dirty!

The prince wandered away, crestfallen. And when the princess returned to the farm that evening, she was disguised in her rags once more.

Time passed, but the prince could not stop thinking of the lovely girl whom he had glimpsed in the mountains. He grew thinner day by day. His parents begged him to tell them what the matter was, but the prince dared not, as he was sure they would laugh and not take him seriously.

"Perhaps he is lonely," the queen wondered.

"Maybe it is time to find him a wife," the king suggested.

So they sent out a proclamation, and beautiful maidens came from far and wide in the hope of marrying the prince. Soon, every young woman of suitable age in the kingdom had been to the palace – but the prince had turned them all away. And still he was sad and ill, getting weaker each day. Finally, he murmured: "The only girl I will marry is the shepherdess who works at the farm over the mountains." The king and queen thought this was very odd, but they were so desperate for their son to get well that they were willing to do anything. So they sent for her...

The princess was terribly embarrassed to be brought into the palace and presented to the king and queen in her scruffy shepherdess's rags. She twisted her hands in

her smock and hung her head in shame.

"But surely our son can't wish to marry her," the king couldn't help remarking, "she's just a shepherdess!"

"And a dirty one too!" the queen added.

Then the poor girl summoned up her courage. "Your Majesties," she said, "please give me some water and leave me alone in a room for a few minutes."

The puzzled king and queen did as she asked. When she came before them again, clean and dressed in her robes and jewels, she looked so beautiful that they could see she was a princess before she even told them herself.

When she was brought before the prince, he at once recognized the beautiful shepherdess he had glimpsed in the mountains, and his heart leapt with joy! He begged her to marry him, and he was so kind and earnest that the princess agreed. Then, she told him her story...

The prince was as good-hearted as the princess. "We must ask your father to our wedding," he insisted, taking her hand. "Let us hope that his heart softens and he will come."

Little did the couple know, the princess's father had regretted his harsh words as soon as she left the castle. He had sent out servants to seek her throughout the land – but they had all returned with no news. Sadly, the king had come to the conclusion that he had lost his daughter forever.

So imagine his great joy when he heard that she was living, and about to marry! He travelled to the prince's palace at once, taking his elder daughter with him.

At the wedding feast, on the orders of the bride, the king was served all his food cooked without salt. There was no salt cellar on his table either. The princess watched him make faces at the poor taste of the food and eat very little of it. Then she approached him and

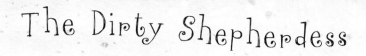

asked: "Is the food not to your liking, father?"

"No," he sighed. "The dishes are obviously carefully cooked, but they are all dreadfully tasteless."

"Well, I told you father, how important salt is! And yet, when I compared you to salt, to show how much I loved you, you shouted at me and banished me!"

Then the king and his daughter hugged each other and he begged her forgiveness. And they all lived happily ever after, with salt on the table at every meal.

MAGICAL MAIDENS

The Twelve Dancing Princesses

Retold from the Grimm brothers'
version of a German folk tale

There was once a king who had twelve beautiful daughters. They slept in twelve beds all in one room and when they went to sleep, the door was shut and locked. However, every morning their shoes were found to be quite worn through, as if they had been danced in all night. The princesses said they did not know how it happened, and no one had been able to find out.

So the king made it known to all the land that any man who could discover the secret would have whichever princess he liked best as his wife – and be the next king, too. But whoever tried and did not succeed would be thrown into the dungeons.

It wasn't long before a prince came riding boldly up to the castle. He was welcomed warmly and in the evening was taken to the chamber which joined the princesses' bedroom. The eldest princess brought him a cup of wine, then returned to her sisters in their bedroom. The king then locked the door and left them all alone for the night. The prince kept his chamber door open, thinking he would watch the princesses and find out what was happening. But alas, his eyes drooped, his head nodded, and he fell fast asleep! When he awoke in the morning, the princesses' shoes were full of holes as usual, no one was any the wiser – and it was off to the dungeons for him.

After the prince came several other daring young men, but not one of them managed to stay awake to keep an eye on the princesses – and down they went to the dungeons.

Now it so happened that a brave soldier, who had been wounded in battle so could no longer fight, was passing through the land. On the road he met an old woman, who told him about the twelve princesses and asked if he would like to marry one and become king. "Just take care not to drink any of the wine the eldest princess brings you, and as soon as she leaves you pretend to be fast asleep," she told the soldier. Then she gave him a cloak, and said, "As soon as you put this on you will become invisible. You will then be able to follow the princesses wherever they go."

When the soldier heard this, he was determined to try his luck, so he thanked the mysterious old woman and made his way to the castle. He was as well received as the others, and when evening came he was led to the chamber that joined the princesses' bedroom. The eldest princess brought him a cup of wine – but the soldier poured it away when she wasn't looking. Then the king bade them goodnight and locked them in. The soldier lay down, and in a little while he began to snore loudly, as if he was fast asleep.

When the twelve princesses heard this, they began to giggle. They got out of their beds and dressed themselves in their finest clothes, chatting and laughing excitedly. However, the youngest said to the others, "I don't know why, but I feel very uneasy – I am sure something is going to go wrong tonight."

"Don't worry," said the eldest princess. "Nothing ever goes wrong. I gave the soldier the sleeping potion and it's worked just like it worked on all the others – he's not going to wake up for hours!"

When all the princesses were ready, the eldest clapped her hands smartly and her bed flipped up against the wall to reveal a trapdoor in the floor. The soldier opened one eye slightly and saw the princesses going down through the trapdoor one after another. As soon as the last had disappeared – the youngest – he jumped up, put on the cloak that the old woman had given him, and followed them down into a steeply winding tunnel. In his hurry not to lose them, he trod on the gown of the youngest princess! "Someone has stepped on my gown!" she cried.

"You silly thing!" said the eldest. "You probably just snagged it on a nail in the wall." So on they all went…

At the end of the tunnel they came out onto a beautiful grove of trees with diamond leaves that glittered and sparkled. The soldier decided to take a sprig away with him, as a souvenir. But as he broke off a little branch it made a loud *SNAP!* "Did you hear that noise? That's never happened before," the youngest princess said in alarm.

"Stop imagining things and hurry up!" the eldest replied impatiently.

They went on till they came to a great lake, where there sat twelve little boats. Standing next to the water's edge were twelve handsome princes, waiting for the princesses. Joyfully, the princesses ran to them, and each couple got into a boat and began rowing across the lake. The soldier stepped into the same boat as the youngest princess. When they were halfway across the lake, her prince remarked: "I do not know why, but the boat seems very heavy today. I am rowing with all my might, but we're going awfully slowly."

Finally, they reached the other side of the lake, where there stood a mighty castle. It was

lit up with coloured lanterns, as for a party, and merry music filled the air. The couples hurried into the castle and began to dance. The soldier, still invisible, danced with them too. They danced and danced till three o'clock in the morning! By then, the princesses' shoes were all worn out. The princes rowed them back over the lake (but this time the soldier placed himself in the boat with the eldest princess). Then the princesses said goodbye and promised to come again the next night.

Back through the grove and the tunnel they raced – but the soldier ran on before the princesses and lay down on his bed. As the twelve tired sisters came up through the trapdoor, they heard him snoring. "See, everything is fine," whispered the eldest

princess to the youngest. They changed into
their nightdresses and went to bed.

In the morning, the soldier was brought

before the king. The twelve princesses stood outside with their ears pressed to the door, to hear what he would say.

"Why are my twelve daughters' shoes worn through night after night?" the king asked.

The soldier answered, "Your daughters dance with twelve princes in a castle underground." And he told the king all that had happened, and showed him the diamond twig he had taken from the grove.

The king called for the princesses at once and asked them whether what the soldier said was true. Of course, the young ladies realized that their secret was out and confessed everything.

So, true to his word, the king asked the soldier which of the princesses he would choose for his wife. The soldier answered that he would like to marry the youngest, for she was the one who had nearly guessed he was there. They were soon married, and every day of their lives the soldier made sure that she and her sisters had music and dancing to keep them happy.

The Tsarevna Frog

Retold from Verra Xenophontovna Kalamatiano
de Blumenthal's version of a Russian fairytale

*L*ong ago in Russia, there lived a king and queen who had three sons, all handsome and brave. One day, the king told them: "Each of you take your bow and fire an arrow – wherever it falls, you must find a wife."

The arrow of the eldest prince fell into the garden of a noble family. The arrow of the second prince fell into the porch of a rich merchant. And the arrow of the youngest prince, who was called Ivan Tsarevitch, fell into a swamp where it was caught by a frog. And so the princes were married: the eldest to a regal noblewoman, the second to a graceful merchant's daughter, and the youngest to a croaking frog – for he would not disobey his father.

After a while the king called his three sons to him. "Have each of your wives bake a loaf of bread by tomorrow morning," he told them.

Ivan returned home with a heavy heart.

"*Croak! Croak!* Dear husband of mine, why are you so sad?" the frog asked gently.

"The Tsar, my father, wants you to bake a loaf of bread by tomorrow," Ivan explained.

"Do not worry, just go to bed," said the frog.

Once Ivan was asleep, his wife threw off her frogskin and turned into a beautiful, sweet princess – Vassilissa by name.

In the morning, Ivan awoke with the crowing of the cockerel. To his astonishment, a loaf was made – and a marvellous one. On the outside, it was decorated with pretty figures, animals, trees and flowers, and on the inside it was white as snow and light as a feather.

The king was extremely pleased, and praised the frog's loaf most highly.

"Now there is another task," said the Tsar with a smile. "Have each of your wives weave a rug by tomorrow."

Ivan returned home in dismay once more.

"*Croak! Croak!* Dear husband of mine, why are you so sad?" asked the frog.

"How can I not be? The Tsar, my father, has ordered you to weave a rug by tomorrow."

"Do not worry, just go to bed," comforted the frog.

Ivan did so – and again the frog turned into the lovely Princess Vassilissa.

In the morning, when the cockerel crowed, Ivan awoke to find the most beautiful silk rug before him, woven of silver and gold threads.

The Tsar was mightily pleased and admired this rug much more than the others. Then he issued a new order – he wished to see the wives of his three handsome sons for himself, the very next day.

Ivan returned home in despair.

"*Croak! Croak!* Dear husband of mine, why are you so sad?" asked the frog.

"My father, the Tsar, has ordered my brothers and I to present our wives to him. Now tell me, how dare I take you, a frog?"

"Come, come, it's not all that bad," answered the frog. "You go on ahead on your own and I will follow you."

So the next day, Ivan arrived on his own at the palace, exceedingly worried. His two brothers were already there with their wives, who were bright and cheerful and dressed in rich garments. Both of the happy bridegrooms began to make fun of Ivan and ask where his warty wife was.

Just then, a magnificent carriage drawn by six splendid horses sped up to the entrance of the palace, with Princess Vassilissa inside it. She looked beautiful beyond all description. The princess stepped lightly out of the carriage and gently stretched out her hand to her astonished husband. Speechless, Ivan led her to see the king, who was utterly charmed.

That evening, the king held a great feast in honour of his sons and their wives. All night, everyone's eyes were on the enchanting Princess Vassilissa – and none more than her

happy husband, Ivan. In a quiet moment, he quickly ran home, found the frogskin, and burnt it in the fire.

After the feast, when the princess found that the skin was gone, her beautiful face grew sad and her bright eyes filled with tears. "Oh, dear Ivan, what have you done?" she cried. "I was under a curse to wear the ugly frogskin for three years – and the time was nearly up. Soon, we could have been happy together forever. Now I must bid you goodbye." And Princess Vassilissa vanished.

Ivan wept bitterly for many days. Then at last he resolved to search until he found her, and set off on his quest.

After many weeks of wandering Ivan came across an old man, who listened to his sad tale, and said: "I pity you and want to help you. Here is a magic ball. Follow the ball wherever it rolls – and do not be afraid."

Ivan Tsarevitch thanked the good old man, and began to follow his new guide, the ball. It rolled down paths and roads, over fields and streams, up hills and down valleys, over plains and through forests...

One day, while following the ball across a wide meadow filled with flowers, Ivan came across a bear. He took his bow and was about to kill it, but the bear suddenly spoke to him. "Do not kill me, kind prince! I may one day be of use to you," it said in a gruff voice. So Ivan did not shoot the bear.

Neither did he shoot a beautiful white duck he saw flying overhead, nor a big grey hare he noticed leaping by. Both animals promised they would be of use to him, so he spared them and continued on his way. And when Ivan followed the ball to a river where a big fish lay gasping on the bank, he kindly scooped it up and put it back in the water – and it was saved.

All this time, he followed the ball as it rolled along. Eventually, it brought him to a strange little hut standing on tiny hen's feet. It was the home of Baba Yaga, an extremely ugly witch.

"Ho! Ivan Tsarevitch!" the witch hissed. "I know all about your lost princess. She is held prisoner at the palace of Kostshei the Deathless, who is a most terrible demon. He watches her day and night, and no one can conquer him. His death depends on a magic needle. That needle lies within a hare, within a box, hidden in the branches of an old oak tree. That tree is watched over by Kostshei as closely as he guards the princess herself – more closely than any of his treasure."

The witch told Ivan where to find the oak tree and he hurried there at once. But when he found the tree he simply stood looking up at it, not knowing what to do. Suddenly, to his surprise, the bear he had spared came galloping up to him. In a second the bear had uprooted the tree, causing the box to tumble out of the branches onto the ground, breaking into many pieces.

Immediately, a hare jumped out of the box and bounded away. But another hare, the one Ivan had spared, went running after it, caught it and tore it to pieces.

Out of the hare there flew a large grey duck, which flapped so high it almost disappeared in the clouds. But the beautiful white duck Ivan had spared appeared and followed the bird. It struck the grey duck, and an egg fell from its body.

That egg tumbled into the deep sea. All of a sudden a big fish came swimming along, the same fish Ivan had saved, with the egg held in its mouth.

How happy Ivan was to take the egg! He broke it and found the needle inside, the magic needle upon which everything depended. As he did, the evil Kostshei lost his strength and power forever. When Ivan reached Kostshei's palace, he entered without challenge and stabbed the demon with the magic needle, killing him. Then he found his own dear wife, his beautiful Princess Vassilissa. They travelled home and lived happily for the rest of their lives, always being most kind to animals.

The Princess Bear

Retold from Andrew Lang's
version of an old fairytale

Once upon a time there was a king who had only one child – a daughter. He was so proud and so fond of her, that he lived in constant terror of something harmful happening to her. So he forbade her to step outside the palace, forcing her to live the life of a prisoner.

The princess did not like this at all – and by the time she was grown up, she found it unbearable. One day, she complained about it very bitterly to one of her ladies-in-waiting. Now, this lady-in-waiting was a witch, though the king did not know it. For some time she listened and tried to soothe the princess, but when she saw that she would not be comforted, she told her: "O princess, I can help you – just do as I say. Go to your father and ask him to give you a wooden wheelbarrow, and a bear's skin. When you have got them, bring them to me."

The princess did as the witch-maiden advised her. The king was greatly astonished when he heard her strange request, but he granted it nonetheless.

When the lady-in-waiting saw the wheelbarrow, she touched it with her magic wand. "There!" she told the princess. "I have enchanted it so it will take you wherever you want to go, in the twinkling of an eye." Then she touched the skin with her magic wand. "Put that over you and you will take on the form of a bear. No one will recognize you," the witch-maiden said. "Take this, just in case," she added, handing the princess her wand.

The excited princess took the wand, wrapped herself in the bear's skin and seated herself in the wheelbarrow. In a second, she found herself far away from the palace and moving rapidly through a great forest. Here, she stopped the barrow with a flick of the wand that the witch had shown her, and went wandering through a grove of flowers.

Now it so happened that the prince of that country was hunting with his dogs in the forest. When he caught sight of the bear he called his dogs, hounding them on to attack it. But the girl, seeing what danger she was in,

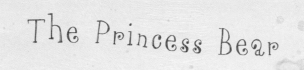

cried out, "Help! Call off your dogs, or they will kill me!"

The prince called his dogs back at once. He was very startled to hear words coming from

a bear! As he looked more closely at the trembling creature, he was quite charmed by it. "Will you come with me?" he asked. "I will take you to my home – you will be safe there."

"I will come gladly," replied the bear and, seating herself on the wheelbarrow again, it at once began to move in the direction of the prince's palace.

You may imagine the surprise of the prince's mother when she saw her son return accompanied by a bear in a wheelbarrow! But when the bear set about doing the housework better than any servant, the queen made the creature most welcome. So the bear stayed and lived in the palace quite contentedly.

Now there came a time when a great festival was being held in the palace of a neighbouring king. "This evening there is to be a great ball – it should be wonderful," the prince said to his mother one day.

"Go and dance and enjoy yourself," the queen replied.

So later that evening, the prince set off. Once he was gone, the princess ran to the wheelbarrow and threw off the bear's skin. She touched them both with the magic wand that the witch-maiden had given her. In a moment the skin was changed into an exquisite ballgown woven out of moonbeams, and the wheelbarrow was changed into a carriage drawn by two prancing steeds.

The princess put on the beautiful gown, stepped into the carriage, and rode to the grand entrance of the palace. When she entered the ballroom, she looked so lovely that everyone wondered who she was. From the moment the prince saw her, he fell desperately in love. All evening, he would dance with no one else but the beautiful stranger – although she would not say a word to him.

When the ball was over, the princess rode away in her carriage at full speed. She wished to get home in time to change her ballgown back into the bear's skin and the carriage into the wheelbarrow, before anyone discovered who she was.

The prince spurred on his horse and rode after her, but the carriage was too swift for him to follow. When he reached his home he could talk to his mother of nothing else but the beautiful stranger. And the princess bear smiled to herself.

The next evening there was a second ball. The young prince hurried off to it eagerly, for he was desperate to see the lovely girl again.

Sure enough, as the music struck up and the first dance began, the beautiful stranger

entered the ballroom. She looked even more radiant, for this time her dress was woven out of the rays of the sun. All evening the prince danced with her, though she wouldn't say a word. And when the ball was over she dashed to her carriage and was off again like the wind, too fast to follow.

When the prince reached his home, he could not stop telling his mother all about the lovely girl. And again, the princess bear smiled secretly to herself.

The next evening, there was a third and final ball. The prince arrived as early as possible – and again the princess followed. This time, she wore a dress of starlight and she looked dazzling! The prince danced with her all night, and although she stayed completely silent, he managed to entice her to wear his ring on her finger. However, when the ball was over, she dashed off once again and he lost her, just as before.

When the prince reached his home he said to his mother, "I am so much in love with that girl, I do not know what is to become of me. I might go mad, for I haven't a clue where to find her. I don't even know her name!"

Then the princess bear chuckled to herself and fetched the prince a dish of soup to warm and cheer him. However, before she took it to him she dropped in the ring he had given her at the ball.

The prince began

to eat his soup very slowly, for he was sad at heart and all his thoughts were on the mysterious princess. But at last he saw the ring at the bottom of the dish. He was speechless with shock.

Then he noticed the bear standing beside him, looking at him with gentle, beseeching eyes. Something in the way the creature looked at him made him say: "I don't believe you are a bear after all! Take off that skin right now!"

The princess bear shed her skin, leaving a beautiful girl standing before him in a dress of starlight. The prince saw that she was the stranger with whom he had fallen so deeply in love. Overjoyed, he led her to his mother and the princess told them both her story. The queen was charmed by her and rejoiced that her son had fallen in love with such a lovely young lady. So the prince and princess were married, and lived happily for many years, reigning wisely over their kingdom.

The Princess and the Demon

A retelling of Katharine Pyle's version
of an ancient Persian fairytale

There was once a man who was very
unlucky, and had lost all his money. So
he sailed to a far-off land to seek his fortune.
He was travelling down a road one day
when he came to a place where three men
were quarrelling fiercely over an old turban, a
carpet and a sword. The men told him they
were brothers, and that when their father died
he had left them these three things. Whoever

placed the turban on his head would at once
become invisible. Whoever sat on the carpet
had only to wish himself somewhere and the
carpet would carry him there in a flash. And
whoever wielded the sword could cut through
anything – no magic could stand against it.

"We all want these things!" cried one of the

men. "You must settle the argument and decide which of us should have them."

"Very well," said the young man, "but before I decide I must try out each of the objects and see whether what you have told me is true."

So he took the sword and cut through a rock as easily as if it had been cheese. Next, he put the turban on his head and became invisible. Then he spread the carpet on the ground – and wished himself far away, where the brothers would never find him!

Immediately the young man found himself on the outskirts of a large city. He stepped from the carpet and rolled it up with the sword and turban hidden inside. Then he sauntered into the city, whistling happily. In the busy streets he heard talk of the king who lived there. The king had a beautiful daughter who disappeared from the castle every night. Each morning, she refused to tell her father where she had been or how she disappeared. So the king had offered a reward to anyone who could find out the truth – half of the kingdom and the hand of the princess in marriage, too. However, if anyone tried and failed they would be thrown into the king's deepest dungeon.

The lad made up his mind to try. He strode straight to the castle and was shown in to see the king at once. That very evening, he was taken to a high tower and left in a corridor near a room there. As he waited, the princess came up the staircase. She did not even glance at him, but she was so beautiful that his heart leapt within him. The princess opened the door to the room. Quickly, the lad picked up the carpet and sword, put on the turban of invisibility and slipped in after her.

Inside the room, the walls were lined with iron and there was only one door and one window. The princess locked the door and suddenly, to the young man's horror, a huge, ugly demon appeared outside the window.

"Sit upon my head," growled the demon, "we must leave straight away." The princess climbed out of the window and onto a huge shield which the demon had strapped to his head. But the lad was quick and sprang out behind her. "How heavy you seem today, princess," cried the demon.

"I don't know what you mean!" answered the princess indignantly.

The demon flew away through the night, so fast that the lad had trouble keeping from falling off.

After a while, they came to a garden where

the trees were made of silver and gold. As they passed through, the young man stretched out his hand and broke off a twig, and put it in his shirt. But the tree began to sigh and moan, and the princess cried, "Someone else is here in the garden!"

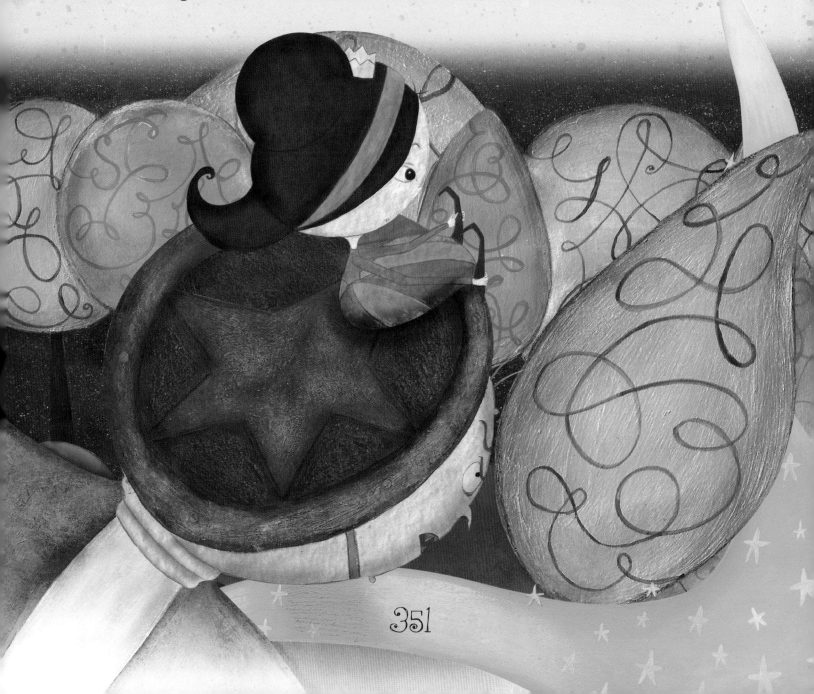

"That's impossible," answered the demon, but he flew on faster than before.

Soon after, they came to a magnificent palace and the demon flew in through a vast entrance. The princess and the young man leapt down from the shield and the demon immediately vanished.

The princess opened a huge door and went through into a grand hall, with the lad close behind her. And there on a throne sat a hideous demon king! He was huge and ugly, and much more fearsome than the first.

The demon king strode over and bent low to greet the princess with a kiss – but the lad stepped between them and gave the demon such a push that he almost fell over!

"Why do you push me away?" bellowed the demon king at the princess, enraged.

The princess began to tremble. "I did not

push you," she insisted. "I am sure somebody must be in the room with us."

The demon king looked all around, but he couldn't see anybody. Then he called a slave to bring the princess the jewelled slippers she always wore at the palace.

Into the hall came the slave, with the jewelled slippers on a golden cushion. The princess took one and put it on, but at the same time the lad took the other and slipped it into his shirt. The princess and the demon hunted everywhere, but they could not find it.

"How careless you are!" roared the demon. "Never mind, we will have a sherbet together."

He clapped his hands and another slave appeared, bearing two crystal goblets full of sherbet. The princess took one goblet and the demon the other. Just as they were about to drink, the lad dashed the crystal goblet from

the princess's hand so that it fell upon the marble floor and shattered, spilling all the sherbet. Then he picked up a splinter of the crystal and hid it in his shirt. The demon king was now furious, but also very alarmed.

"What did I tell you!" cried the princess, shaking so much she could hardly stand. "Something is wrong, terribly wrong!"

"Yes, I can see that for myself," said the demon king. "You must leave immediately."

The first demon was summoned, the princess mounted the shield in haste, and away they flew. But this time the lad did not fly with them. He waited until they were gone, and then he drew the sword and slashed the demon king's head from his shoulders.

The lad then seated himself upon the carpet and wished himself back in the tower, outside the iron room. And there he was in a flash, long before the demon had brought the princess back, although he flew as swiftly as the wind. The lad took off the turban, rolled up the carpet and lay down as though he were asleep.

Next morning, the princess called the guards and ordered them to take the young man away to the dungeon.

"Wait!" he cried. "First, I demand to be brought before the king."

The princess could not refuse this, so they went to see the king, and the young man began to tell his story. When he got to the part where the demon had come and flown away with the princess, she turned first as red as blood and then as pale as death. "It is not true!" she cried, but the king ordered her to be silent.

Then the lad told how they had flown through the garden of gold and silver trees. "It is all a wicked lie," claimed the princess, but the lad showed the twig to the king as proof.

After that, he told how they had entered the palace, and of the demon king and the shattered goblet. He produced the splinter of crystal from his shirt, so the king knew it was all true. The princess, meanwhile, looked more and more fearful.

Last of all, he explained that the princess had left the palace but that he had stayed behind and cut off the demon's head.

To his astonishment, when the princess heard this she gave a shriek of joy. "Then you have saved me!" she cried. "I no longer have to be the demon king's slave!"

Then it was her turn to tell her story. She had been walking in the palace gardens one night when the demon king had seen her and fallen in love with her. He had cast an enchantment to gain power over her, so that every night she was forced to visit him in his palace, and never reveal the truth to anyone. But now he was dead, she was free!

When the king heard this, he rejoiced. It was announced to the kingdom that a wedding was to take place, and everybody was happy. Although happiest of all were the princess and the young man, as they had fallen deeply in love.

The Three Daughters of King O'Hara

Retold from Jeremiah Curtin's version of an Irish folk tale

There was once a king in Ireland whose name was Coluath O'Hara, and he had three daughters.

Once, when the king was away from home, the eldest princess decided that she'd like to be married. So she put on her father's magic cloak and wished for a kind and handsome man to be her husband. No sooner had she taken off the cloak than a golden coach arrived at the castle, and sitting in it was the most handsome man she had ever laid eyes on. She went away with him at once.

When the second princess saw what had happened, she too put on the magic cloak and wished for a kind and handsome man to be her husband. She took off the cloak and straightaway a silver coach arrived, and sitting in it a man nearly as good as the first. She went away with him immediately.

Then the youngest princess put on the magic cloak. She wished for the best white dog in the world. Presently he arrived, in a coach of gleaming glass. The princess went away with him at once.

When the king came home he was enraged to discover what had happened – particularly to hear that his youngest daughter had gone off with a dog!

Meanwhile, at her new home, the first princess had discovered that her husband was only a man in the daytime. At night, he became a seal. The second princess discovered the same – her husband was a man in the daytime but took the form of a seal at night.

However, the youngest princess found that her husband was only a white dog in the daytime. At night, he shed his dog skin and transformed into the most handsome man in the world!

After some time had passed, the king invited the three princesses to visit him for a feast. He had calmed down and was very glad at the thought of seeing his children. However, the queen was still upset and thought it a great disgrace that her youngest daughter would be coming with a dog. When the pair arrived, the queen wanted to banish the white dog to the castle yard, but the princess insisted he sat beside her at the feast.

When all the guests had gone, the princesses and their husbands went to their own rooms in the castle. Late in the night, when everyone was asleep, the suspicious queen crept in to each one. She was horrified at the sight of the seals! However, when she stole into her youngest daughter's room, she was amazed to see sleeping there the most handsome man she had ever laid eyes on. Then the queen noticed the skin of the white dog, lying on the floor. She carried it away and flung it off the highest turret of the castle, into the dark sea below. There, it was ripped apart by the waves.

The moment the skin reached the water, the husband of the youngest princess woke and sprang up, which woke her too. He was very angry and sad, and told her: "I am under an enchantment – if I had been able to spend a whole night with you under your father's roof, I would have got back my own form for good, and could have stayed with you as a man. Now I will remain a man, but I must leave you forever…"

He ran out of the castle and sped away as fast as his legs could carry him – but the youngest princess followed, and did not let him out of her sight.

They ran for the rest of the night and the whole of the next day. Then at nightfall they came to a house. "Go inside and stay here till morning," the man said to the princess. "I'll pass the night outside where I am."

So the youngest princess went in. The mistress of the house welcomed her, gave her a good supper and showed her to a comfortable bed. In the morning, as the princess was about to leave, the woman gave her a gift – a whistle. "If you are ever in trouble or despair, put this whistle to your mouth and blow on it," the woman said.

The princess thanked her and went outside to her husband.

"Go back to your father's castle," he said.

"I will not," she replied, "I will follow you for as long as I can."

They ran a little way off to a grassy mound, then he turned to her and said with great sadness, "Today I must be gone from you forever. It is the fairy queen of Tir na n-Og who enchanted me – and now I must go down to her kingdom and marry her. I have no power and can do nothing against her cruel spell. So farewell, you will never see me again in this upper world."

The young man went a few steps to some bulrushes, pulled up a handful, and disappeared into the opening where the rushes had been.

And so the princess was left all alone in the

countryside, sitting on the little mound. She broke down and wept, for she didn't know what to do. But she soon made a decision. Gathering her courage, she went over to the bulrushes, pulled up a handful and followed her husband, not stopping until she reached the fairy country.

In the distance, the princess could see a city, above which rose the gleaming spires of a palace. So she set off towards it. In the streets of the city, she heard the fairy people talk of how the queen had married a new husband that very day! Filled with despair, the princess put the whistle to her mouth and blew. At that moment, all the birds of the air flew to her from every direction.

"How can I get my husband back from the fairy queen? Should I kill her – and can I do it?" the princess asked the birds.

"It is very hard to kill her," came the reply from the bird king. "There is no one in all of Tir na n-Og who is able to take the queen's life but her own husband. He must climb the mountain behind the palace and enter the dark cave at the top. Once there, he must find a jewelled box. It contains the queen's soul, so if he destroys the box, she will die."

The princess thought for a moment, then asked the bird king to take a message for her to the queen. He was glad to help, for everyone in Tir na n-Og thought the queen was evil and cruel, and would be glad to be rid of her.

The message told the queen that a princess was in her land, who owned a whistle that could call all the birds of the air. The princess offered to give the queen the whistle if she could send a letter to the queen's husband.

In no time at all the bird king brought back an answer – the queen, of course, could not resist the whistle. So he returned to the palace carrying the whistle, which he delivered to the queen, and a letter from the princess, which he ensured a servant delivered straight to the queen's husband.

In the letter, the princess explained to her beloved how she had followed him to Tir na n-Og. She told him that only he had the power to kill the queen, and described how he could do it.

As soon as he read the letter, the young man's heart was filled with joy. That night, when the queen was sleeping, he crept stealthily out of the palace and climbed the steep, towering mountain behind. It took him many hours, but at last he reached the dark cave and entered it, trembling. He began to

search for the jewelled box, and eventually found it in the darkest depths of the cave. Without hesitation, he smashed it to pieces with a rock. At that instant, the soul inside was destroyed, and the fairy queen died.

Then the young man ran like the wind to his faithful princess, and embraced her joyfully. He gave a great feast for the fairy people, at which everyone rejoiced and celebrated. The couple never left Tir na n-Og and, as far as I know, are living there still in peace and happiness.

Princess Pepperina

Retold from Flora Annie Steel's
version of an Indian fairytale

A songbird once flew out of the forest to a high-walled garden. Tall mango-trees shaded it on all sides and many brightly-coloured flowers and fruits grew within. But there was no sign of life inside its walls – no birds nor butterflies, only silence and the sweet perfume of flowers.

The songbird flew to the middle of the garden and found a single pepper plant growing there. Among the polished leaves shone a single green pepper, gleaming like an emerald.

The songbird's companion loved to eat green pepper, so he was delighted. He flew back into the forest and fetched her to the garden, where she at once began to feast on the delicious plant.

Now the garden belonged to a genie, and the pepper was his favourite plant. The genie was fast asleep in a summer-house, for he generally stayed awake for seventeen years and then slept for seventeen years. Yet he began to have a nightmare in which his prize green pepper was being pecked to pieces! Becoming restless, he awoke – just after the songbirds had flown away, leaving a glittering emerald-green egg beneath the pepper plant.

As usual upon waking, the genie yawned

and stretched and went to see how his pet pepper plant was getting on. How sad and furious he was to find it pecked to pieces! He could not imagine what had done the mischief, as he knew that no bird, insect, nor beast lived in the garden.

"Some dreadful thing from the horrid outside world must have stolen in whilst I slept," muttered the genie to himself, and immediately began to search for the intruder. He found nothing, however, but the glittering green egg. He was astonished and took it back to his summer-house. There, he put it away carefully in a little cupboard.

Every day, the genie went and looked at the egg, sighing over the thought of his lost pepper. Until one morning – lo and behold! – the egg had disappeared, and in its place sat the loveliest young girl! She was tiny, dressed from

Princess Pepperina

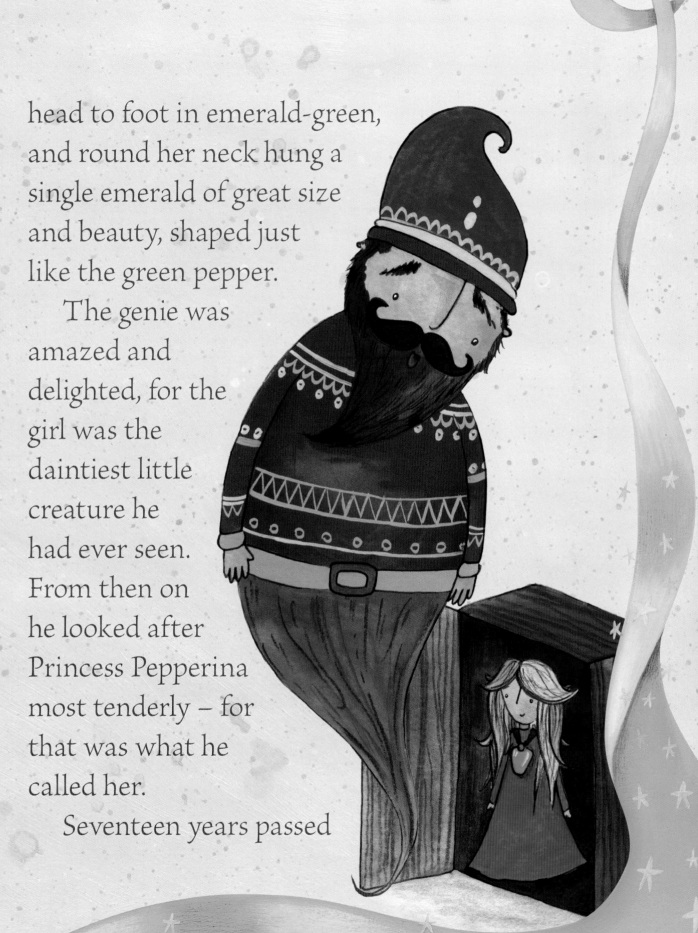

head to foot in emerald-green, and round her neck hung a single emerald of great size and beauty, shaped just like the green pepper.

The genie was amazed and delighted, for the girl was the daintiest little creature he had ever seen. From then on he looked after Princess Pepperina most tenderly – for that was what he called her.

Seventeen years passed

by in the beautiful garden and it came time for the genie to go to sleep again. He was very worried about what would happen to his princess when he was no longer able to take care of her. But it so happened that, before he had nodded off, a king and his minister who were on a hunting expedition came upon the high-walled garden. Curious to see what was inside, they climbed over the wall. There, they found the lovely Princess Pepperina seated by the pepper plant.

After talking to her for a while, the king had fallen deeply in love, and begged her to be his wife. But the princess hung her head, saying, "You must ask the genie who owns this garden – only he has an unfortunate habit of eating men sometimes."

However, the princess could not help thinking that the king was the handsomest and most splendid young man in the world. So she told him to hide away in the garden and that she would speak to the genie for him.

No sooner had the genie appeared than he began to sniff about, crying, "Fee! Fa! Fum! I smell the blood of a man!"

Princess Pepperina soothed him, saying, "Dear genie, you may eat me if you like, for there is no one else here." The genie laughed and kissed her. Then the princess cunningly sighed and wondered aloud what she would do in the walled garden alone while he was asleep. At this, the genie became greatly troubled. He declared that he wished he knew of a nobleman to marry her and look after her – but he was sure there was none worthy nor handsome enough for Princess Pepperina.

Hearing this, the princess seized her opportunity. She clapped her hands and the splendid young king appeared from a thicket. The genie was shocked, but even he had to admit that they made a perfect couple. So he consented to their marriage – which was held in great

haste, for the genie was beginning to nod and yawn. Yet when it came to saying goodbye to his dear little princess, the genie wept so much that the tears kept him awake. It was only when Princess Pepperina left to travel to her new home with her husband that he could finally fall asleep, although the thought of his dear little princess remained.

During the years which followed, the young king remained passionately in love with his beautiful bride. But the other women in the palace were very jealous of her, especially after she had a baby – the most lovely young prince imaginable. They were determined to get rid of her, and spent many hours plotting how they might do this – some even wanted to kill her.

Finally, they hit upon a plan. One night, the wicked creatures crept into the queen's room and stole the infant prince from his little crib. Early next morning they hurried to the king, weeping and wailing. "Look!" they cried. "The beautiful wife you love so much is nothing but an evil witch. She has used your son in a magic spell and he is gone, nowhere to be found!"

The king was grief-stricken, because he loved both his son and his wife deeply. Yet Princess Pepperina could not explain how the baby had disappeared, so he banished her from the kingdom forever. The lovely young queen left the palace utterly heartbroken, while the wicked women rejoiced at their evil success.

At long last, Princess Pepperina found her way back home to the high-walled garden, where she began to sob bitterly. "Oh, how I wish I had my baby boy!" she cried. Little did she know that the emerald (which she still wore around her neck) was in fact a magic talisman. No sooner had she uttered her wish than the beautiful little prince was back in her arms.

At the same time, back in the palace, the sorrowful king was listening to two songbirds chirp outside his window. As he listened, he was suddenly able to understand them – they were talking of how the wicked women of the palace had

stolen his young son and betrayed his beautiful queen!

Upon hearing this the king, with a rapidly beating heart, galloped away to the high-walled garden at once. There he found Princess Pepperina, smiling and cradling their little son in her arms. He begged her to return home with him, vowing he would never again distrust her, and would put all the wicked women to death. But Princess Pepperina refused, saying she would prefer to live always within the garden, where she was sure that she and the prince would be safe.

"Just so!" cried the genie, who had at that very moment awakened from his seventeen years' sleep. "Here you shall live – and I will live with you!"

So he built the king and queen a magnificent palace, where they lived with their son most happily ever after, and the genie enjoyed their company for the rest of his waking days.

The End